Your Exciting
Middle
Years

Your Exciting Middle Years

John C. Cooper
and
Rachel Conrad Wahlberg

Word Books, Publisher
Waco, Texas

First Printing, June 1976
Second Printing, August 1976

YOUR EXCITING MIDDLE YEARS

Quotations are from the Revised Standard Version of the Bible,
copyright 1946, 1952, © 1971, 1973
by the Division of Christian Education of the
National Council of the Churches of Christ in the U.S.A.,
and are used by permission.
Chapter one is an excerpt from *Religion After Forty* © 1973 by
John Charles Cooper.
We are grateful to Pilgrim Press (United Church Press) Philadelphia, Pennsylvania, for granting permission to reprint this portion.

ISBN #0–87680–857–7

Library of Congress catalog card number: 76–2858

Printed in the United States of America

contents

preface

Welcome to a serious reflection upon the meaning of middle life. The authors of this book invite you to join them on a journey of self-discovery, an opportunity to become aware of the challenge, problems, and joys of mature adulthood.

This book is the product of a joint effort to understand the meaning of our (Rachel and John's) own experience as Christians. It goes beyond the simple report of two person's lives, however, the discussion here does reflect two lifetimes of ministry to people as Christian writers, as teacher, pastor, and counselors.

Your Exciting Middle Years is written to help us come to a recognition of who we are, where we have been, where we are now; to examine our problems and the solutions to these problems suggested by a mature Christian faith and to offer clues as to where we might be going.

This book is also designed to point out and recommend to you the inexhaustible riches of the Christian faith, for every age of humanity and for every year of a person's life. We hope that as you read you will be studying the Bible and other Christian resources. Where the Bible is not directly referred to in the text, its relevance is assumed.

This book is also designed to help us discover how we and fellow Christians might interact together to tap the spiritual riches of Christian faith. Rachel and I believe that we were born to love God and enjoy him forever—in youth, middle life, old age, and in eternity. Sometimes we forget that and become confused, weary, depressed, unhappy. This is not necessary if we keep open to God and to one another.

This book may also help uncover where we hurt, where we are weak, where we are strong, and give us a clearer idea of what our true values are. Sometimes we become discouraged and depressed when we get confused about the direction of our lives and begin to evaluate ourselves and our accomplishments by inappropriate standards. If this is the case with any of us, we hope to discover the situation and help in achieving a solution to the problem.

Besides being written to the general audience, *Your Exciting Middle Years* is a reading book for a nine-session course for groups in classes. There are three cassettes, a response manual, and a leader's guide (besides the book), all produced by Creative Resources, P.O. Box 1790, Waco, Texas 76703. For information on a thirty-day free review service, call collect to 817/ 772–7650 and ask for a sales representative of the telephone marketing division.

It is hoped that the experiences we will have together will make us more able to cope with the difficulties of life in a time when many of the old traditions are passing, generational conflict is a fact, and the church's ability to help people is questioned. This book is our invitation to you—people in the middle—to stop, look, and listen both ways—toward the younger and the older generations—and to look more deeply into yourselves and your faith for aid in living through these exciting middle years.

JOHN C. COOPER

1.

Who's in the Middle?

JOHN C. COOPER

A popular misconception about those of us in our middle years is that we are completely home and work oriented; indeed, almost selfish in our indifference to the affairs of the world around us. While it may be true that some people of limited vision live that way in the 1970s, it is not a correct appraisal of the modern person in middle life. Whether or not we like the events that are going on in our world, most of us keep ourselves well informed of the problems and conditions of the human community at all levels. We also find our lives very much affected by the daily developments in our society. People of all classes, backgrounds, and education read the newspapers and watch the nightly news.

We who are reaching middle age in the 1970s have lived our entire lives in a mass media setting. We came into the world when radio was coming into vogue, and we have marked our development by attendance at increasingly sophisticated motion pictures, radio programs, and since the early fifties by the total communication of television. Living in this omnipresent electronic environment has made our generation in middle life world-conscious. Those among us have very probably served in distant lands and taken active parts in the events that have shaped our world. Consequently, we must understand the world that we have known over our developing decades if we are to understand the kind of individuals we have become, and the kind of spiritual resources we require. Viewed with a historical perspective, the time span between 1930–1974 is a fantastic one politically, economically, philosophically, and religiously.

The Great Depression

For anyone who enters the middle years in the 1970s, the Great Depression is more of a phrase than a very vivid memory, although the experience of growing up during this time has played a very great role in the formation of our characters. Indeed, the chief truth behind the assertion that there was a generation gap a few years ago, largely lies in the different attitudes toward money and the difficulty—or lack of difficulty —of making a living among those who were affected by the depression and those who were not. Even for the majority who never went hungry the possibility of hunger was felt by the parental generation, and this was communicated to the children. It is still an element in the core character of even the most liberated members of our generation. This anxiety was reinforced later by the advent of World War II and the cold war which followed it. Therefore, the alleviation of anxiety is the major religious need of our generation. The economic downturn in the early 1970s has done nothing to relieve us of our anxieties, for we still go to work every day—if we have work—and pay inflated prices for our groceries and other needs.

Challenge and Response, 1939–1945

So much has been written about World War II that we will not take space here to review anything but the most salient factors of the experiences of those years upon the spiritual development of our generation. For those who, like myself, began school in 1939, the beginning of some thirty-five years

of continuous war or the imminent possibility of conflict coin-
cides with our intellectual development. We are who we are
because we have never known what peace really means. I am
not suggesting that all or most of us in middle life are mili-
taristic or extremely conservative, for we are not, but I do suggest that both the liberals and the conservatives among us
respond to situations in the world with an anxiety rooted in
the wartime conditions that have marked most of our lives.

One somewhat opposite but related effect of World War II
on our generation must also be noted. This is the fact that
after the period of disunity in America over our participation
in the war (1939–1941), we were a people sparked by the
tragedy at Pearl Harbor to act together in a unified spirit
seldom seen among us. The impression, gained as school-
children in the early forties, of being a part of a people bent
on a single goal remains with us, as a benchmark against
which we have measured the manifold social events since
1945. Perhaps the quest for self-identity and civic power on
the part of Blacks, then the Mexican–Americans, the American Indians, the women's liberation movement, the student
groups, and the homosexual groups, has seemed more threatening than it actually is because of our subconscious memories
of the unity we thought we obtained during World War II.

This subconscious benchmark has been largely responsible
for the deep distress many of us have felt over social situations
during the last decade. In that way the war that was our
youth has also fed our anxieties. It has also served as a line of
polarization between many over forty and the student generation of today, for whom World War II is only a few chapters
in a modern history book.

Catching Up: The Rise of Affluence

The ashes of World War II were not cold before America
completely demobilized and began a breakneck race to supply
the goods and services demanded by a population which had
acquired more ready cash (by virtue of war work, military

pay, and veterans' benefits) than ever before. The large increase in marriages brought on by the war and the return of
men from the war made for a building boom. Children began
to be born in large numbers, in contrast to the decades of our
generation when the birth rate was low. The technological
developments spurred by wartime needs were turned to the
creation of dozens of new or improved household appliances,
which by the late forties culminated in the birth of the
television age.

Nevertheless, the spread of the new technology probably
would not have been as rapid, or the rise to affluence on the
part of the large middle class (and its increase in size) as
steep, or even as certain, without the reinforcement of our
anxiety by the challenge of the cold war. Somehow we have
tended to forget the years when people built fallout shelters in
their yards and stocked them with supplies, all the while
debating whether or not they would shoot their neighbors if
they tried to get into their shelters with them during an
attack. Those also were the years in which the cold war broke
out into open conflict in Indochina and Korea. The Korean
stalemate fixed our anxiety into a long-range belief in the
inevitability of conflict between the two major powers of the
world, and gave us the unconscious belief that somehow conflict and prosperity were correlated.

An Age of Anxious Emptiness

The postwar period proved to be less filled with happiness
than we had hoped, and the American people turned to
religion for resources to cope with the emptiness and fears of
so-called peace. These were the years of the revival of religion
in which a number of noted evangelists, who are still quite
popular, first came to fame through the mass media. These
were also the years the denominations of every theological
stripe experienced the greatest increase in membership in their
histories. The churches of America welcomed the influx, and
for the first time over half our people became at least nominal

members of churches and synagogues. But apparently the theology presented by the churches was not adequate to deal with the anxiety and inner needs of the people. Such deep-felt anxieties that had their bases in the deprivation of the depression and the threats of war, coupled with the opposite but related feeling of emptiness that had come with the achievement of affluence, could be adequately dealt with only by a deeply philosophical and sound biblical theology. Philosophy was out of fashion, however, and the Bible was not necessarily the focus of the theology of any of the churches, whether fundamentalist or liberal. Men and women turned to other avenues for release, while maintaining their church membership. The divorce rate began to soar, a sure sign of social dissatisfaction and of a personal search for relief. Alcoholism grew, followed in the 1960s by an increase in the misuse of drugs. Suicide maintained a steady popularity, for the revival religion was simply too shallow to bear up the broken center of an individual or a society.

The business of religion was good in America during the years 1946–1961, but then it began to slip. After the early sixties the increasing American involvement in Vietnam and the increasingly violence-filled turmoil of civil rights activity and campus unrest exposed the vacuum at the core of much of the church's teaching and practice. Now such competing faiths as Zen Buddhism, varieties of Hinduism, and numerous occult practices arose in response to the population's spiritual anxiety and emptiness.

There was one movement which began quietly as long ago as the fifties, though it has only recently surfaced and caught the public eye. It was the very deep search for spiritual meaning begun by people of our generation within the beleaguered churches. This movement of renewal began with twin roots. One root was a form of liturgical and congregational revival that stressed the intimacy of small cell groups within the larger church, often fashioning itself around a celebration of the Lord's Supper. This became known as the underground church in the middle and late sixties, when it became associated with involvement in Christian social action.

The second movement toward spiritual renewal is the current phenomenon known as the neo-Pentecostal revival. It is within this movement in the church that much energy is now being expended in the search for an answer to our anxiety and emptiness. While some members of the youth counterculture, like the so-called "Jesus People," are also part of the charismatic or neo-Pentecostal movement, men and women of our generation as well as persons older than ourselves seem to be the leaders and chief supporters of this reemphasis on speaking in tongues, witness bearing, and faith healing. People of all ages appear to be drawn to this emphasis on the Spirit— just as another large group of people seem to be drawn to the occult—as the Age of Aquarius deepens and the world is found to be no closer to physical or spiritual peace.

An Age of Spiritual and Social Crucifixion

Any outline of the political and social stresses of the last twenty-five years would include the coming of the civil rights movement and the violence and racial tensions the opposition to it triggered in our culture. The shock waves of this long-overdue social reorganization produced the murders of innocent Blacks in the deep South, the execution of civil rights workers by right-wing groups, and the assassination of Martin Luther King, Jr., in 1968. These shock waves are still being felt in potently political ways in the antibusing movements that helped to determine the outcome of the 1972 presidential election and continue to trouble our major cities today.

Spiritual crucifixion became a reality for most people in the nation with the eruption of violence as a common feature of American life. The assassination of President Kennedy, followed by the murders of Robert Kennedy, Dr. King, and later the attempt on the life of George Wallace, have revealed the deep undercurrent of sickness that can produce violence in many Americans. The fact that both liberals and a conservative leader have been the victims of violence show that one's politics does not save him from our society's ills.

Finally, we must mention the Vietnam War—the longest war in American history, with an official starting date in 1961 and an official ending in 1973—as perhaps the most disturbing political event of our mature years. Much of our internal crucifixion is directly related to the involvement of the country in this overseas adventure. The radical religious movement and the civil rights movement merged in protest against the war, with Martin Luther King, Jr., becoming an outspoken opponent of the administration before his death.

The wave of campus disruption that characterized the late 1960s—culminating in Kent State—and which called into question the very reason for being of the American university system, was due to Vietnam. Here the shoe began to pinch, for it was people of our age group who filled the professors' chairs on these campuses and who had children in their teens who were affected by the public hatred directed toward students.

This wave of protest and reaction on the campus angered and disturbed both our blue and white collar families, since they did not understand it. The present quiet on campus is, therefore, welcomed by them.

An Age of Emotion

Our experiences produced a mass market for a new morality and created an open season for the spread of new religious forms. Much of what our generation had simply retained in the way of institutional membership and as a standard of conduct was thrown into serious question by the events following World War II. But no widespread philosophical positions emerged to gather together the disinherited and the disenchanted.

During the sixties the only source of inspiration and challenge seemed to come from the leaders of the civil rights and antiwar groups. The religious aspect of what was essentially a spiritual struggle contented itself with the echoing of political beliefs. This was not entirely true, but those religious thinkers who did seek to give depth to the search for spiritual roots and goals were little heeded by the public at large. Religious leaders were prominent to the degree that they spoke out in shocking or radically political terms. Joseph Fletcher and Bishop Pike, with their offer of a new morality, seem to have offered more specious justification for our present actions than guidance for further improvement.

Because there was no intellectual infrastructure for our response to the crisis of our time, the human spirit naturally turned to the emotions for comfort, escape, release, and even salvation. This was not such a new phenomenon in American life, since the challenge of civilizing the frontier community was largely met by the emotional instruments of the revivalist. The response to total war had previously been the creation of propaganda based as much on feeling as on fact. The response to the anxieties of the depression had been the emotionalism of drunkenness and the creation of the cult of the gangster in the Prohibition era.

It was no surprise, then, that the sixties witnessed an outburst of feeling-based movements. This was the generation of our youthful maturity when we created the T-group, sensitivity training, the weekend marathon, the group analysis experience culminating in transactional analysis. It was not the teen-agers but the people of our generation who sought salvation through the group process based more on feeling than on insight.

These feeling-based activities paralleled, were influenced by, and in some sense were responses to the growing subculture of drug abuse that characterized the sixties. Drug misuse began slowly with the use of marijuana borrowed from the musician's subculture and experimentation with heroin taken from the underworld. This influence was strengthened when women abused diet pills, businessmen abused pep pills, and people of all classes became dependent on tranquilizers and sleeping pills. This drug orientation of our generation influenced the student generation behind us, and many young people discovered drugs through stealing pills from their own parents' medicine cabinets. Our youngsters learn from us to depend on uppers and downers.

The human potentiality revolution is a response of our generation to a feeling that the world is slipping away into chaos. Since the exterior forces of traditional meaning have not been satisfying, the remaining alternative is to try to find the world within oneself. This basic spiritual and psychological involution is at the root of the interest in the occult, of the human potentiality developmental psychologies, of drug experimentation, and of the neo-Pentecostal emphasis on spirituality. If we look around us or within us we see this search for self-meaning going on in all quarters of our society.

It is because of this search for meaning that we have helped to create this kind of world. Now it is time to turn to the question: What kind of persons have we become, because of the journey we have made?

The Persons We Have Become

The 1970s are an exciting period in which to hit middle life. Those of us who have made it this far are younger, more excited and exciting, and much more involved in all manner of interests than we were in our twenties. Considering the events of the world during our lifetime it is amazing just to be alive. We have passed through war, economic illness, national emergency, and the threat of nuclear war on our way to this prime time of life. We have learned to live with one eye on the social barometer of group unrest in the way our rural ancestors learned to live with one eye on the weather.

The anxiety and emptiness that we feel in our lives express themselves in the multitude of marital crises. As a group we have made and broken a large number of marriages. The increase in the absolute number of divorces in our society has been due both to the increasing acceptance of divorce as a reasonable terminus of many marriages, and to the crises and strains through which we have passed. One of the characteristics of our generation is the phenomenon of remarriage. Few people end a marriage and remain single. Large numbers of us not only have wives or husbands and children at home, but also ex-spouses and other families living in another location. A number of us have "my children," "your children," and "our children." What this situation is doing to all our children is a problem that we will someday have to face.

Children form a very large part of our lives. Our generation had a good many children. We were married before the Pill became a part of everyday life. Whereas our parents, psychologically squeezed by the depression, generally had small families—making us a rather select group—we, fueled by the anxieties produced by war, have had larger families.

While our large postwar families may have been built as much through unconscious accident as conscious design, it is fair to say that our lives revolve around our children. The Pill came too late for us, and in any event the experience of war gave us such a deep need to achieve some kind of immortality through our children that we wanted them anyway. At the time of the birth of my fourth child, a prominent sociologist was making a presentation on the population explosion at the University of Chicago. I was a graduate student there and had a pocketful of cigars to give to my friends. One friend laughingly suggested that I offer the sociologist a cigar and tell him what it was for. I did and found that he was incensed and refused to take it, saying, "It's people like you that make our work so hard." Perhaps we will turn out to be the last generation with big families.

Some psychologists say that there are no sharp transitions from young adulthood to middle age. This may well be true for those who are busy in work that absorbs much of their time and energy. For the man in middle life busy with an eight-hour-a-day job or harried with the responsibility of a management position, there is little time to reflect and to mark the passing of the calendar.

For the woman also, the constant rush of keeping house, holding a job (or both), may make her oblivious of the transition from young adulthood to middle life. Exercise, good diet, and medical care preserve the woman's health and attractiveness much longer than was the case with our grandparents. The fact that the woman in middle life still thinks of herself as young and very aware of her sexuality is reflected in the television advertisement "You're not getting older, you're getting better."

However, the woman of our age group, like her husband, is driven by many anxieties and she senses some very real empty places within her. The same flight from anxiety into activity that impels her husband to excel at moneymaking and climbing higher on the social ladder also causes the wife to overinvolve herself in many civic, school, and church activities. The average middle-class household of our generation more closely resembles the corporation in which so many of our men work than it does the families of our childhood. Not only does the husband have many demands upon his time from his work, civic clubs, politics, and church, but the wife also has many mornings and evenings filled with meetings devoted to everything from ecology and congressional legislation to becoming a better Sunday school teacher. Add to this the multitude of activities of our boys and girls, with their daily basketball games, music lessons, dental appointments, and dances, and we have the kind of activity that if diagramed by an efficiency expert would seem characteristic of a business concern.

There has been a great deal of study by psychologists and sociologists on the development of children and youth, and in recent years much attention has been paid to the problems of the elderly. But perhaps the true forgotten majority in America is the generation over thirty-five and under sixty-five. We are the generation that is now doing most of the work of the country and paying most of the taxes. We are the ones paying the increased payroll deductions for larger Social Security benefits. Perhaps it is only our built-in anxiety that keeps us running and running to attain the goals of security and prestige without questioning the validity of those goals as the student generation has done.

But while the man of our generation may get lost in his work and overlook the passing from youth to age, nature puts up a signal to women: the menopause. While menopause need not be traumatic and usually is not, such a physical shift to the end of worrying about childbearing is bound to have psychological and spiritual effects. One's outlook on the future changes during the move into middle life.

Just What Is Middle Life?

Ledford J. Bischof, in his 1969 monograph *Adult Psychology,* reports: "The middle years as a span of life suffer from statistical vagueness. The person approaching middle life strives to delay its advent until the age of forty."

Dr. Bischof quotes the psychologist Levine, who holds that the span from thirty-six to fifty-five is the closest approximation to middle age in a life-span of seventy years. Developmental psychology would call the period twenty-five to forty the years of middle adulthood, and the period forty to sixty the years of late adulthood. Else Frenkel says that the years from birth to age forty are the construction years, ages forty to fifty the culmination period, and the years sixty and over a reduction period.

Ours is a generation overstimulated by concern for health. We live in a culture whose actual rulers are not the philosopher-kings of Plato but the physician-priests of Hippocrates. As a group we have been pinched and poked, innoculated and exercised, nourished and dieted, and all the while propagandized to watch for the danger signs of cancer by the medical and paramedical professions. Only our children have had more medical care than we have.

But our generation has desired health largely because health is identified with youth. It is the fear of old age and death (as well as disease) that impels us. The young Buddha learned of these three plagues long ago, according to Asian legend, and drove himself to attain release from their terrors.

Imagine the situation of suddenly being forced by your body to the conclusion that you are growing older in a society that worships youth—in the abstract, though perhaps not in the grubby particular. Our culture worships youth. All our styles, our songs, our stars are centered upon youth and its pansexuality.

I am quite sympathetic with the desire to remain young and healthy. Perhaps few people really want to grow older. But nature lies largely outside our desires and wishes. We must live within the limits of life and within the sublimits that fall within it. Not fully accepting entry into middle life can play havoc with the changing time perspectives that attention to the reality of our lives demands. We miss many opportunities for mental, social, and spiritual development because we do not face up to our real age and situation in life. James E. Birren, writing in *The Psychology of Aging,* declares that one of the major sources of frustration in our society is definitely age-related. It is an age status system that idealizes youth.

We need, therefore, to allow ourselves to be the persons we have become.

Coming to Terms with Our Age

The value of attaining maturity lies in the possibility of creating something new, of moving from a position of the son to that of the father, of the daughter to the mother. We can take satisfaction in having grown up and having graduated to a full maturity if we exert ourselves to think, to plan, and to build.

For some this creativity expresses itself solely in the accumulation of property. However, we are shallow individuals indeed if there is no other measure of our accomplishment than the financial. We do sell ourselves short when, as in the case of most of us, we look over our financial picture and find it not very bright. In measuring our accomplishments there is more to weigh than money alone. We need to keep in mind the children we have reared, the ideas we have promoted, the causes we have supported, the people we have befriended, the houses we have built, the flowers we have grown, and the very experiences we have lived through in order to receive a clear picture of the worth of our life.

The Stages of Life

Truth and fact faced squarely somehow set us spiritually free. But facts which are turned away from, become stronger and stronger prisons of maladjustment. The freedom that facing the truth brings is not a freedom from worry and care but a freedom to undertake other more appropriate tasks—like growing up.

The psychologist Erik Erikson has taken Freud's psycho-analytic concepts and projected them beyond the infant and child levels of behavior to cover maturity and old age. He postulates eight stages of ego development that correspond to eight periods of life which he believes he observes in the fully developed human being. Erikson expresses these stages as polar opposites: the first term being the positive or healthy achievement and the second or opposite term being the negative or psychotic failure. Erikson's assumption is that of Freud: that physical growth into maturity does not automatically resolve the tensions between these extremes; therefore size, weight, and chronological age are not the only marks of true maturity. Indeed, progress through life is a continuum from one stage to the next, with the ever-present possibility that one may fail to complete the challenge of one stage or the other and hence fall into emotional problems.

Erikson's eight stages are:

1. Trust versus distrust (early infancy).
2. Autonomy versus doubt and shame (later infancy).
3. Initiative versus guilt (early childhood).

4. Industry versus inferiority (middle childhood).
5. Ego identity versus role diffusion (adolescence).
6. Intimacy versus isolation (early adulthood).
7. Generativity versus ego stagnation (middle adulthood).
8. Integrity versus despair (late adulthood).

Thus Erikson's way of measuring maturity, and a way our generation might measure itself, is to check whether we have resolved the conflict in each of these eight stages of ego development. Particularly for our stage of life it is important that our ego identity is well fixed, that we have achieved a degree of intimacy with others and are now ready to allow creativity to flower in our lives, becoming, in middle adulthood, generative rather than stagnant in our ego development. If this challenge or task can be met, then we may say that we are mature. In the terms of another psychologist, Abraham Maslow, we will have then become fully self-actualized persons. It may be beneficial to our generation, which has so often become conformist, to know the various characteristics that Maslow sees as the marks of self-actualization or maturity:

1. Oriented realistically, efficient perception, good judge of others, quick to judge them.
2. Accepts self and others and the world for what they actually are, not for what he wishes they would be, not hypocritical.
3. High degree of spontaneity, unaffected in behavior, acts natural, may appear unconventional.
4. Problem-centered not self-centered, works on problem not self, not very introspective.
5. Inclined to be detached, great need for privacy at times, not entirely dependent on others, can amuse self, can detach self and concentrate alone, may appear aloof to others.
6. Autonomous within self and independent, dependent on self, serene.
7. Fresh appreciation of people and world, not

dulled—not "I've been there before" but "every sunset is as beautiful as the first," "ten-thousandth baby as miraculous as the first."

8. Somewhat mystical or profound inner experiences, seems out of this world at times.

9. Identifies strongly with fellowman, but does not join in empathetic way, has older-brother personality, wants to help, truly interested in the welfare of others.

10. Deep and intimate relationship with only very few, has special friends or small circle of friends, highly selective in friends, gives absolutely to them, easily touched and moved by children.

11. Strong democratically oriented values, can relate and learn from rich or poor, acquaintances' class or race or position not important.

12. Understands difference between means to achieve a goal and the rightful ends to be achieved, strongly ethical and highly moral, though may differ with popular idea of right and wrong, focuses on ends and purposes.

13. Philosophical and whimsical inner-motivated sense of humor, does not laugh at cruelty, strong sense of incongruity, does not tell jokes as jokester but rather sees jokes in everyday things spontaneously.

14. Tremendous capacity to be creative, one of the most universal capacities in all self-actualized people, no special talent but new touches to life, creativeness of child, fresh way of doing things.

15. Swims against mainstream, very open to new experiences, resistant to conformity.

Probably a larger number of people in our generation

come closer to meeting some of these criteria than members of our parents' generation. However, if a majority of us were close to these desirable traits there would have been no need for the rise of the counterculture, with its new mentality, among the younger generation.

This list of criteria for maturity applies to all of life, of course, and not just to those reaching forty. Perhaps there is truth in the remark that there is but one major crisis in reaching middle age and that is being middle-aged.

Self-Fulfillment

Men and women who have reached mid-life should already have discovered their personal identity and now should be moving toward the completion of that identity by achieving personal integrity. While our integrity is judged by others on the basis of the consistency of our character and our personal honesty, this is but the outer expression of an inner sense of self-fulfillment. This is an inner affirmation of things as they have been and are which gives a basic satisfaction conducive to happiness.

I would suggest that Charles Dickens' story *A Christmas Carol*, stripped of its sentimentality, gives us a very incisive picture of an individual who was mature only in the chronological sense. But he came to psychological and social maturity, and hence to happiness, because of a creative vision of his own mortality. A part of becoming mature, and a good part of the story of what kind of individuals we have become, lies in creatively facing up to the fact of our own death.

Dickens shows us Scrooge as an old man who had no psychological affinity with other men and no social sense. He was still piling up money although he had little time left to enjoy it. Until the ghost came to haunt his dreams, there was in him no sense of the shortness of life. The visions made him aware of the death of others and then of his own death. Upon coming to an appreciation of the weakness that is inherent in all of us, Scrooge was enabled to turn his greatest failure, his selfish accumulation of money, into his greatest strength, the ability to help others. The story ends happily because Scrooge triumphs, not over others, but over himself, precisely by a creative rechanneling of his weakness.

Most of us do not qualify as Scrooges. We have had to scramble for a buck. We lived on the pittance of the GI bill while struggling to complete our education or we started on the job at the lowest salary paid. Long before the call to the "greening" of America and return to the simple life, we cut our own hair, repaired our own cars, sewed our own pants, doctored our own illnesses. Many of us still do those things. The reality of being poor has not left most of us. Sometimes we look at a thirteen-cent stamp uncomprehendingly, remembering how upset we were when first-class postage was raised to four cents.

But we are not a generation of Archie Bunkers either. Our generation was the backbone of the civil rights movement and of every worthy cause that came along. As a group we have never been stingy with our money or benighted by ancient hatreds. Still respectful of the dollar, we are less likely to treat it as a god than is sometimes suggested. But like Scrooge we are likely to be hung up on money, and even more likely not to take seriously the prospect of death.

Freud suggested that most people find it hard to accept the reality of their own deaths. Other people die. We know that, for by now we have known many people who are gone, but the existential fact that we are going too is hard to grasp.

Accepting Our Death as Part of Our Life

Just here our little excursion into the recognition of graying hair and growing older merges into a very definitely religious area: the acceptance of our death as part of our life (as Paul Tillich put it) and a serious recognition of that aspect of faith usually referred to as immortality.

A long time ago, when I was very old at the age of nineteen, for I had just survived two tours of combat with the First

Marine Division in Korea, in 1950 and 1951, this thought struck me with telling force. I realized that I was going to die—not just that I might die if a mortar shell fell on me or a machine gun sprayed the road where I was walking, but regardless of all that, in time I was going to die anyway. I recall this experience of insight as more terrifying than all the strain, pain, and hundreds of narrow escapes that I suffered in Korea, narrow escapes that put me in the naval hospital in Japan twice, one of which left me partially crippled for life. All that effort, fear, and pain had been experienced like a bad dream that I continually prayed would be over, when I would be back in the childhood I had so lately left—a time that knew no reality of death. This experience of insight (or the achievement of maturity) took place only after I escaped the situation of continual danger and entered again the state of war's being "over." Only then, as time passed and I was a university student did I quietly come to see that nothing had really changed, nothing would ever be "over" until I was "over." Minister or lay person, such thoughts come to each of us who is honest with himself, whether early or late. For those fortunate enough to have escaped spiritual trauma from war, accident, or disease, the time of reckoning usually comes around age forty.

When it comes, let it come. Go with the flow of feeling that comes from your most personal (as well as biological) depths. Go with the terror, the anxiety that Luther graphically described in his early writing; go with the despair. Do not think that hiding these feelings, blocking them off, laughing them away, is an answer. But go with this crisis of your existence only to the point that these feelings are fully expressed. Get it all out at one time, look at it from many angles and refuse yourself the bittersweet pleasure-pain of playing the pseudonihilistic "I'm going to die" game over and over again. This recognition of our finitude, this kind of grappling with our mortality is a sign of maturity and mental health. But repetition of this crisis of middle life every time we grow a little fatigued, ill, depressed, or drunk is a lack of maturity and is only mental morbidity. Once you really know that you are going to die—then you are ready for the greatest message of the Christian faith: the person who has faith in Christ shall live. Though you are as good as dead, through Christ you may enter an eternal dimension of life in which terms like beginning and ending, birth and death have no meaning.

The Faiths We Have Tried

It seems like a long time ago sometimes—and like only last week most of the time—that I began teaching religion in college in the 1950s. Fresh from war and graduate school I encountered the phenomenon that meets us every day in the classroom and study, as well as every Sunday at worship services: baby-fat faith.

Baby-fat faith is the term I devised to cover the religious "beliefs" many people in our generation hold. It is made up of the maxims and dogmas we picked up in Sunday school and from our parents. Such baby fat melts away quickly under any form of exercise such as concentrated biblical study. When the fat melts away we can feel strong and fresh, or we can wallow and drown in its oil, but we can never put it back on again.

Some commentators would refer to this phenomenon as other people's faith, our parents' or our pastor's faith. This is a good term, too, for what is involved is the loss of other people's beliefs and the acquisition of our own.

Sunday School Religion

In the twentieth-century world there has been a fantastic increase in the sophistication of education in all areas. It is not uncommon for men and women to be competent in several fields and have a more or less deep appreciation of the complexities of politics, social problems, and military problems. However, the very same people may be illiterate in the religious area.

The concrete or Sunday school stage of religious faith is characterized by a literalistic retelling of Bible stories without any attempt to relate them to our life here and now in a systematic way. This may explain two seemingly unconnected but related phenomena. One is the heavy attraction of biblicalism and conservatism for people in middle life, and the other is the desertion of the church by intellectuals and workers who became politically and socially aware.

However, being stopped at the concrete stage of religion may also be due to an inadequate attention to the higher possibilities and deeper meanings of Scripture. I once heard an atheist remark that he liked his religious people to be conservative for it made his efforts to wean people away from Christianity much easier than if he had to try to counter the arguments of more liberal ministers.

Joining the Church

For many of us, joining the church came as a matter of course because of our family background. In the more liturgical churches, we were sent to catechism classes and were confirmed at about fourteen. In the free churches there may have been some peer group pressure as well as adult expectation brought to bear on us that culminated in a conversion experience marked by adult baptism. The experience of our generation seems to be that most of us joined the church attended by our parents, and some of us joined churches through the influence of others, although our parents were not good churchmen. Ultimately, the majority of us in youth and young adulthood dropped away from close communion with the church only to return after marriage and the coming of children.

Falling Away in Service and/or College

In the armed forces many of the men of our generation fell away from the concrete stage of religion. The need to come to grips with social problems and situations of a complex moral

nature made the static, either/or Sunday school morality we
had been taught untenable. It soon became clear that the
real world was a more complex place than our small-town
values-enshrined-in-conservatism were designed to handle.
It was easy to slide into the cynicism of Napoleon, who once
remarked that God was always on the side of the bigger
battalions. Yet, rather than pushing men completely into
unbelief, the general experience of war seems to be to nudge
them toward a more tolerant, open attitude toward religion.
A kind of "religion in general" springs up.

For those who escaped war and overseas service in our time,
there was the experience of college. What was uncritically
accepted at home was often critically attacked on campus.

Having to face up to the deeper meaning of religion and
to the meaninglessness of much peripheral material in religion
is a good, not a bad, thing. However, our generation did not
have the opportunity to embrace the fundamentalism that
characterizes the Jesus movement today. The old standbys
that have gained so much for the Jesus movement, Campus
Crusade and Youth for Christ, were on the job in the fifties,
but they were ahead of their time.

I can still recall when an ex-paratrooper on our hall was
converted. He came up and began to "witness," leaving everyone confused. He could not have been regarded as more
strange if he had dressed in women's clothes. Gradually he
drifted away and was forgotten. Our generation was not a
good market for traditional religion, at that time, by a wide
margin.

Suburban Religion

While our college days did little to call us back into the
traditionally religious fold, not many of us became atheists.
We lived by the religion-in-general and existential ethic of
our earlier years. Some of us affiliated with the church. Some
of us even entered the clergy. For most in our generation,

however, the decision to join the church came after marriage and the coming of children.

The church in America was expanding in the middle fifties, growing at a rate it had never before experienced. The pressures to join congregations in such suburbs were high. "Home missionaries" beat the bushes of every residential street. (I know—I was one.) New church buildings sprang up all over.

This was, for all too many, a change from a vague religion in general to a not much more profound religion of convenience. We joined the nearest congregation of our own (racial) color and supported the church of our choice.

I do not mean that such an expansion of church membership did not do some people a lot of good. Gradually, the bright young pastors and their educational efforts deepened the commitment and understanding of many people in our generation.

But if it was too easy to become part of the church in our early adult years, it was just as easy to drift away. Long weekends and increased incomes made weekend vacations the rule and absence from church the regular life-style of our growing families. As long as the church did not demand very much, things were fine. Then history caught up with us and time invaded the cathedral. Martin Luther King, Jr., and other clergymen began to apply a mature interpretation of Christian faith and morality to our social situation. Most lay people were either oblivious of the dawn of a new religious period or were against the "radicals." Suddenly the deadest place in town became the center of action.

Large numbers of men and women in our generation are still upset over this period of church history. For many, there was a real love of the church but no understanding of the new movements.

The quiet forties gave way to the chaotic sixties. Some of us dropped out of the spiritual race altogether, others of us began the favorite game of the sixties and seventies: spiritual exploring.

Spiritual Exploring

Our generation passed into the sixties like dough pushed through a spaghetti press: we went in together in one lump and separated into many individual strands. Some of us stayed right where we were, others moved into the center of the action: civil rights first and later the antiwar movement. We rang the changes on our own souls or went with the flow of the forces around us.

This tendency ran through its course to an apex around 1970, and probably involved only a fraction of our generation other than some clergymen and college instructors. For the most part the twin themes of civil rights and antiwar sentiments were hard for our generation to understand or to accept.

Another model of spiritual seeking has been the frank embracing of hedonism, which is popularly symbolized by the Playboy philosophy. Essentially, the urge to escape into sensuality is but one more form of escape from the problems of the world. While some form of immorality is found in every generation, it is interesting to note that in ours it has taken the form of a critique of the family and of an expressed desire to attempt a rehabilitation of marriage. The many experiments with group sex, "swinging" or wife-swapping, are not fully understood unless they are recognized as attempts to create alternative philosophies of life in order to explore new ways of relating to human beings. The fact is that the swinging experiments fail simply because they are so individualistic that they can produce little that is enduring through time.

The church and other groups that have criticized the hedonism of today have taken the shallowest approach by criticizing this phenomenon as immoral. The proper response is to point to its short-term durability and its inability to build structures that will last throughout the lifetime of its practitioners. Does it or does it not inhibit the full development of the personality? Can it possibly be the basis for the creation of forms of social life that include younger people and the aged as well as the unattractive in middle life?

The Need for Something More

Today many people in congregations of all communions are breaking through the wall of concrete religion. Intellectually, this is accomplished by increased Bible study, cottage meetings, and attendance at lay schools of theology. Spiritually, it is being achieved by the intense experience of prayer meetings, charismatic congresses, and faith healing sessions. This rise of neo-Pentecostalism represents the last stage yet on the journey of exploring the field of spirituality that characterizes our generation.

The Freedom and Security We Seek

In 1965, I was a visiting lecturer at a layman's summer school of theology, where I presented the case for Christian social activism. I encountered a good deal of resistance, since the students were people of thirty-five and older who came from the midwestern United States. One man was particularly opposed and engaged me in violent argument night and day. He seemed to reject categorically any social dimension to the gospel beyond simple charity. After ten days I left the school and forgot all about this "hardnose."

In the fall of 1971 I found myself teaching in the general area where my old opponent lived. I had forgotten him completely, however, until one afternoon the phone rang. The "hardnose" identified himself, reminded me of our past encounter, and told me that I had troubled his mind for years after our meeting. He said he had eventually been "converted" and was now a leading fighter for social justice in his city. He had changed his mind and found a challenging new commitment to his religion in middle life.

Reaching middle life for our generation does not have to be simply a matter of becoming "set in our way." It can often be a time of deep upheaval and various kinds of "conversions." The church, and in a larger sense Christian faith itself, becomes a matter of increasing importance to us. Some of us move toward the stabilizing and inspiring influences of the organized church, while others begin to feel a pinch in the soul from such a connection. My friend, who moved from conservatism to social activism, illustrates a motion toward a larger spiritual sphere, a move toward a commitment to freedom.

What We Need and Don't Need

Men and women in the middle years need a sense of meaning in their lives. Even people who have more or less successfully met the challenges of each period of their lives and who have strong identities may find their meaning patterns shaken as they face up to the fact that while they had been moving upward until now, they must look to a long slow decline from now on.

Our decline into old age and eventual death is quite gentle and will last a long time.

Considering the reality of our situation, we do not need a religion that seeks to cover up with saccharine emotional dogmas or with abstract philosophizing the challenges that face us. We do need to be helped to understand ourselves, our children, and our society, and to be given the opportunity to deepen our wisdom, faith, and love as our years go by. We need the comfort and support of a deepening faith in almighty God. We need this emotionally, to be sure, but intellectually as well.

Faith in God

"Have Faith in God," Jesus once told a man of our own ages (Mark 11:22). What is this faith?

Faith is essentially confidence. It is trust. Primarily it is not intellectual assent to certain propositions or dogmas. One may give assent to ideas logically presented to him, yet never feel moved, as a total person, to participate in that idea. Faith as trust, on the other hand, may be deeply placed in that which cannot be logically described or proved beyond question. We act on our feelings. Faith in a fact, William James once observed, may be necessary to a fact being proven later, to be a fact—just as we cannot be absolutely sure that a tree trunk over a stream will hold us until we work up the courage and confidence to cross that tree trunk and look back on it from the other side.

A faith like this is not foolishness, but the profoundest kind of floor under our existence, the most viable source of strength that enables us to go on living. It robs us of our impulse to hate, to make invidious distinctions among men, to become loveless and self-satisfied. Such faith makes us the trusted friend and sympathetic counselor each of us, as a parent, wants to be as we grow older. From such a confidence springs the only love that can be wholly constructive: unselfish, impartial love.

We Need a Faith That Is Mature

A mature faith may sound like a slogan, until we consider the stresses and sufferings most of us have had to pass through to reach our present situation. A rereading of the book of Job might give us a few pointers toward a mature faith.

The book of Job stands as a counteraction to the tribal theology of the Old Testament. That theology made the mistake of thinking that the covenant people would be spared suffering and would acquire wealth and security in life. But Job, who was by all accounts a righteous man, suffers terribly. He refuses to pretend that he has been a sinner when he is pushed toward that position by his three comforters. Yet he does not reject God, only the limited idea of God held by his people. In the twenty-fifth verse of chapter nineteen Job, who has known what it is to grow old and experience distress, appeals from the limited idea of God to a more mature faith when he says, "I know that my redeemer lives."

Most of us have probably not had the full experience of suffering as Job did, yet we have met with reversals. If we have come this far with an immature faith that God somehow protects the righteous and prospers the good, then we have been living with our heads under a bucket. The assassinations of Gandhi and Martin Luther King, Jr., the imprisonment of Bonhoeffer in World War II, and the descent of disease and accident upon people without regard to their character should be example enough that faith will not spare us from suffering, although it may make it possible to bear.

Trying to Find Meaning

I have mentioned the problem of anxiety as being one which has plagued our generation. Anxiety comes into being when one is unsure of the stability and permanence of important elements in his life, such as parents, necessary food and shelter, health, social acceptance, and the like. Anxiety is relieved when one experiences what Tillich called acceptance, or what Jung called "centering," or what traditional theology calls salvation.

I would suggest that the religion we need, and the one that many of us are now searching for or engaging in, is one that will "center" and thus give security to our lives. Like Archimedes, the Greek inventor in ancient times, we look at the power, education, and wealth we have acquired as a group, but do not know how we can use it as an instrument to bring about social and inner peace. Archimedes had invented the lever, a powerful tool not unlike our wealth and power, and like us he searched for some way of centering this power so that it could be useful in the maximum sense. He cried out, "Give me a place to stand and I will move the world." The catch was—and is for us, too—that there is no place outside the world on which to stand. Happily, in instances of spiritual healing and in experiences that disrupt one's normal attitude toward the world, many people seem to be finding their centering within Christianity again.

In theology as in physics, people have longed for a place to stand outside the natural order, where we could appreciate the wonder of the works of God. However, having no place to rest the lever of the intellect, the wholly unconcerned world seems to move on, following its own nature, disdaining Archimedes and us. Modern physics and philosophy, more subtle than ancient Greek thought, have pointed out that the observing and acting person in the world does have some rather basic effects upon the world, causing it, as it were, to take account of our very presence.

Werner Heisenberg has shown that the simple act of observation makes a difference in the objective knowledge one can have in atomic physics. The act of observation changes things. Our existential being in the world is itself a part of the world, and human knowledge revolves around the place we stand. We are striving today not to make the universe revolve around ourselves in the physical sense so much as to return to our proper place as the observer of events and the giver of meaning to the great cosmic show. Our generation wants to go beyond the simplicities of so-called objective knowledge to a position that dignifies our meaning and gives us the security we desire as spiritual beings even in a physical universe that may well be governed by random chance.

For most of us there is a willingness to accept vagueness and mystery, for the systems of science, philosophy, and theology seem to have a place for everything in them but us and our problems. Rightly, most of us are unmoved by those who claim to know too much. Yet we are not satisfied by the weak-handed declarations of some thinkers that God is either dead or absent, or that we can do theology in fragments. Our very selves cry out for something whole, satisfying, to which we can cling in the midst of change, decay, and defeat. Old age, poverty, sickness, and death send us, like Buddha, seaching for an ultimate answer, for half measures give release from neither anxiety nor suffering.

What is most interesting about our generation at the present

time is that having walked such strange pathways in reaching
this period of life, we have nevertheless arrived at a very
traditional resting-place. The most recent religious revival is
overwhelmingly traditional and Bible-centered. The Christian
church in all its manifestations has always claimed to have a
simple yet strong message for those in need. The simplicity
of this message however, has often been obscured by many
complexities, and the strength of it has often been weakened
by doubt and a refusal to put the faith into action. The pri-
mary characteristic of religion in the middle years for many
today is a reiterated claim on the simplicity and strength of
the Christian gospel.

2.

What Do You Want to Be?

Rachel Conrad Wahlberg

A well-known coach had decided to give up his football career and take a year to rest and relax, to get in tune with himself, to make some decisions about what he wanted out of life.

Ara Parseghian, head coach for eleven seasons at Notre Dame, said he was not making an impulsive decision. It was something he had been mulling over in his mind for some time. At fifty-one he said he was considering the health and welfare of his family. He also needed time, he said, to "rejuvenate myself emotionally and physically."

Completing a successful season at Notre Dame, he was free to go back to coaching if he wanted to. A man in the news, he received accolades for his winning teams. Financially, he was in good condition.

Why, many people would ask, did he want to give all that up to *think about things* for a year?

In the field of education the one year sabbatical is a common investment of a professor's life in a voluntary reappraisal or rest. A person can travel, study, take courses, lecture—and think. But the idea of "mulling over" for change is not typical of other workers and professionals.

Those of us in the middle years who decide to make a drastic change are often thought to be strange, uptight. Many times society takes a judgmental attitude toward us. What is acceptable for a professor or teacher should be acceptable for other people. There should be no time in our lives when we cannot rethink or grow toward new ventures.

Persons in Transition

Middle age is a puzzling time. When we are young we think that all we have to do is to make some decisions in our twenties and we will be set for life. We believe that if we decide what our goals are, as far as our ambitions and talents are concerned, find a life partner to whom we relate well, and—sound of trumpets and birds singing!—we will live happily ever after.

What seems obvious to us when we are young is that middle-aged people have it made. They seem—from youth's vantage point—to be established. Either they are successful in career, family, and achievement, or else they have settled into a dull sort of routine. When young, it never occurred to us to wonder if our parents had any new options. Could they begin over again? Could they change their style of life? their line of work? Could women launch out into something new when children left home?

When we are young we don't think about options for older people. We are too consumed by our own anxiety and the options before us as youth. Since many of us grew up in the depression years, our generation is especially anxious to be secure, to have an assured income, to know we have savings that can't slip away from us. Indeed, our anxiety from the world of the thirties and forties is such a part of our heritage that we are surprised that young people today are more concerned about whether their life decisions will be meaningful and whether their choices will involve creativity and growth rather than financial security. We were too eager to pin down a good income, perhaps, to be overly concerned about work satisfaction and growth values.

Even with all our anxiety about security, some of our early decisions have not had happy results. As persons in the middle years we see that for many of us the one clear choice we made was not right for us. Or perhaps a clear choice did not overwhelm us. For every person who sees clearly from adolescence the one thing she or he wants to be, there are many others who take one step forward and two steps backward. Perhaps we didn't find the right job or the right family situation until our thirties or forties. Perhaps we never found what seemed "right" for us.

Some of us went into the armed services or rushed into marriage without learning a skill that would be suitable for twenty or thirty years.

Many of us remember talents and interests in our teens that we have never developed or followed through on.

Our values and our life-styles do not remain constant. Some people are finding out today that they have changed their ideas and opinions about many issues. What was important back then is no longer important. Life moves and we move.

Perhaps people in the middle years realize they made decisions that did not work out well. Perhaps a job was not satisfying. They went from one type of work to another . . . and another . . . still seeking. Sometimes a transition has been forced upon them. Sometimes they have sought change.

Perhaps a young man went into service and had a period of forced diversion to think out what he might do next.

Perhaps a young woman and a young man married before the man went off to serve in another country. The relationship did not work out. The two persons were not compatible. They had some aspects of life in common, but not enough for a lasting relationship.

Or, even without a separation, a marital relationship may not have worked out in positive terms. Perhaps the partner one chose was not a happy selection, or the two came from different backgrounds. Maybe they have developed at different rates and in different directions: one has grown and expanded; the other remained static and narrow.

Or again, a couple may be successful in every way, except in personal relations—trusting that marriage would succeed just because there had been a wedding service.

Some transitions diminish us; some challenge us, renew us.

The mayor of a large city was sued for divorce by his wife of over thirty years. She claimed that his political life had taken precedence over the marriage and that for years he had neglected her. Not many years ago Nelson Rockefeller divorced his wife of over thirty years, mother of their five children, and married another woman.

For some people it is difficult to see how a person could make such a major change in the middle years. For others it is understandable that people should not want to continue to tolerate what has become an intolerable situation. They feel they are adult enough, intelligent enough, to adapt to change even after many years of living with a person amidst a growing alienation.

Of course, many of us are not going through a transition during our middle years—at least not a dramatic one such as divorce. But because United States society—with its political and economic turmoil—affects all of us, there is a feeling of anxiety that most of us experience when we reach the middle decades of life.

Another contributing factor is the age consciousness that is a part of our society. Not only have we grown up in a youth-oriented culture, but the advancing age of our population and the problems of older people have made us sensitive to the in-between position we are in.

Bernard Baruch once said, "Old age is always fifteen years older than I am." Psychiatrist James A. Brussel says middle age is "the twilight of one era and the dawn of another."

Approximately 42 million Americans are in the middle years. Professor Bernice L. Neugarten, a University of Chicago psychologist who has studied the middle years, says age comes to educated Americans later than to blue collar workers. A construction worker may feel middle-aged by the time he is thirty-five. But an educated person who has started a family later may feel she or he is not middle-aged until well past forty-five.

Thus, middle age can be regarded as a *state of mind*—as well as a period anywhere from thirty-five to fifty-five.

"I think age consciousness is a disease," says Josephine Lowman, who writes a syndicated column on beauty and health, "which is fatal to vibrant living. It is bad enough at any age but it is down right tragic when it attacks people in the prime of life, and this is just when it usually strikes. . . . Age consciousness has a subtle influence on every facet of their lives. It affects their glands, their personality, their posture, their activities, the way they look, the way they think and even the way they walk. What a waste!"

Each of us can probably think of a person of fifty who apparently feels so old, so much of a has-been that he/she walks in a bent over, sluggish fashion. And again, we may know women and men of eighty or older who have a liveliness to their step and outlook and who defy the label "old person."

Many people in middle age, points out Theodore Irwin, are burdened with a large cluster of worries. "Even though they are in the generation that earns about 60 percent of United States personal income and are the decision makers of society, they're afraid they are doing something wrong."

"I feel my life has been wasted," says a fifty-four-year-old homemaker.

"I wish I could do something of value," says a forty-nine-year-old businessman.

A school teacher of thirty-seven says, "Teaching is a job. I wish I were trained to do something else."

Middle-Age Crunch

Although some of us think the years from thirty-five or

forty on can be exciting, rewarding, beautiful years, others feel that it is a period of "second adolescence."

You may think of this period as the "change of life" or climacteric which is allegedly experienced by men as well as women.

The latest psychiatric thinking is that the biological-psychological impact of "change of life" is much overplayed and affects only the emotionally immature. In a survey of women by Professor Neugarten, 96 percent claimed that menopause was a relatively minor event for them.

"The middle age crisis is triggered by a realization that there is not too much time left," reports Dr. Marjory Lowenthal, social psychologist at the Langley Porter Neuropsychiatric Institute in San Francisco.

"With the clock running out, a middle-ager must decide whether to keep moving outward or to turn inward in order to survive—a sort of death in life. You can keep going or you can spend more and more time in front of the television."

Erik Erikson's eight stages of life development are similar to this view of the middle years. As noted in chapter one, he conceived of the length of life as passing through various stages, in each of which there were tasks to perform, its own challenge to be met.

The period of middle adulthood would be defined as a time to rise to our potential of creativity and productivity—or else slide back into monotony and defeat.

A social scientist, Dr. Orville Brim, president of the Russell Sage foundation, maintains that a "crisis" during middle age implies that something happens and then is all over. He sees instead a continuing discontent with one's self, a continuing search for self esteem.

Behind this search is the rapid period of change, the "future shock" reflected in rapid obsolescence of skills and information. We are faced with the problem of adjusting to what we can do and what we can't do. Those of us who can't accept change look around for other ways of bolstering our self image.

Some men, for instance, become concerned with physical image. They start a vigorous exercise program, get outfitted with a hairpiece or color their hair. Some women spend a lavish amount of time and money in beauty shops, seeking a younger "me," a new image in a physical sense, when the sense of unrest they feel cannot be met in a cosmetic, superficial way.

Trapped between Two Worlds

Some people, according to Brim, have a too-late feeling. We may feel trapped in a job or work that is unrewarding. A job that may have appealed to us at twenty-five is now boring, lacking in challenge. For the woman, a domestic life accepted without question in her twenties may now be coming to an end.

In addition, two generations are facing us. Not only are the young people in the family reaching maturity, but we face decisions that must be made about our own aging parents.

We are caught in the middle in a very real sense. At the one end, we may no longer feel needed by our grown-up children, and on the other, we are fearful and anxious about parents who may be ill, needing medical care, nursing care— or by the death of one or more of our parents.

Dr. Harold Berstein of the University of California School of Medicine says, "Up until this point, people in middle age have almost justified their existence on the basis of their children's needs. They feel a sense of uselessness when forced to admit that their children can take care of themselves."

For those of us who are women, who are we if not the mother-managers of our children's lives? For men, who are you if not the financial provider for your growing children? What if you are no longer needed as parent images?

Older parents present us with a variety of situations:

• Parents who have remained on the farm or in a small town environment, clinging to the ways and values of the past, while their middle-aged children have become more affluent, live in the city and are intensely involved with their own lives.

• Parents who have suffered a loss—loss of health, financial, or some other—who are now dependent on their own children for support and life decisions. Middle-aged sisters and brothers must communicate, share responsibility, often a difficult problem.

• Older parents who are financially secure and in good health, who nevertheless want attention from adult children living across country.

• The single parent who has been widowed. Is she or he capable of living alone? Whose wishes should be determinative? When nursing home care is necessary, who decides? who pays? who helps the parent face the decision?

• The death or critical illness of parents, with its ongoing problems of estate responsibility, funeral decisions, and division of material goods among adult children.

• The widowed parent who has decided to marry again —or, phenomenon of converging Social Security restrictions and less stringent morals—the older parent who decides to live with someone of the opposite sex.

There are other variations of these sample situations. Each of us in the middle years is likely to be faced with critical decisions in relation to the older generation.

Economic Fear

Some of us in the middle years are forced into change by an economic crisis. We fear the loss of a job or a long period of unemployment perhaps more than our younger and even older contemporaries. Unemployment compensation may run out before we find another job. We may never find another position in the field of our training.

Inflated prices have been with us so long that those of us unaccustomed to tight budgets have learned to make difficult choices. Individuals and families are confronted with their own version of crisis. They have been asking: What can we do to protect ourselves? Where can we cut down? How can we change our style of life to conserve?

A young woman in her mid-thirties is anxiously awaiting word from twenty-four job interviews. She has recently achieved her goal of obtaining a master's degree in mental health and mental retardation communications. She has applied for work with various state and local agencies and hopes to be a public relations practitioner for an agency. She finds the job competition fierce and the salary opportunity not the best. She discovers that the type of job she has worked so hard to prepare for is one of the easiest functions to eliminate. Public relations personnel can be reduced drastically or almost eliminated. Sometimes a person already employed is assigned this form of communications.

So the woman anxiously waits, hoping that her careful preparation for the middle years won't be for naught.

Diane Wheeler, a district executive for the Red Cross, notes that the number of volunteers has been dropping in recent months. People who felt they had free time to do volunteer work are now taking jobs for pay. One will call up and say, "I have to go to work, so I can't be a swimming instructor this summer."

At the same time that some of us are losing jobs, others of us who had relied on one family breadwinner or on a small retirement check, are finding ourselves pushed to pay bills and to buy necessities at inflated costs.

Forced to Change Living Styles

People are viewing their lives with a wide angle lens. They see not just the next pay check, or the next vacation, but the possibility that pay checks may stop, and then what?

People are pulling back—on buying cars, on long trips, on unnecessary food, on baking that requires sugar, on giving to church and to charities. There is a spirit of caution.

People are turning to a broader range of transportation—bicycles, motorcycles, smaller cars, city buses. Some cities are providing superior mass transportation. Recently, I was privileged to ride the superfast BART in San Francisco, where the ride from downtown Frisco to my destination in Oakland took sixteen minutes.

Many of us are finding it a challenge to "make do" as our own parents did during depression years. We can make over the old dress, fix the appliance instead of turning it in for a new one after three or four years. We can get the old car repaired instead of falling for high pressure advertising of new cars.

Young people have been ahead of us for several years. For those of us who grew up in the depression, the badge of achievement was to buy new things . . . nice things . . . familiar label goods. To some of our children it is the "in" thing to buy clothing at garage sales and Goodwill stores. The rage for "used" jeans in some college towns has amazed middle-aged parents. The thought of wearing an unknown person's hand-me-downs is abhorrent to us. Yet, youth think it is fun. And the clothing is often better made and more comfortable than some new fashions created out of synthetics.

Two summers ago our seventeen-year-old daughter outfitted herself for three weeks at camp by going to garage sales in our neighborhood. For three dollars she brought home six pairs of shorts, two pairs of jeans and one long-sleeved shirt. She was pleased with herself. "I'm ready for camp," she said.

Because fear about the United States economy has become a major factor in the lives of all of us, people are making fundamental shifts in their life-style they would not have considered a few years ago. They are pulling back, asking more questions, weighing their choices more carefully.

People who have identified themselves for years with a certain life-style and a certain social level are being forced to make reassessments. How can they change in the face of economic troubles? What can they invest in that will give them real security? What is really important to their sense of well being?

We in the middle years, comfortable in our assimilated recruiting, might find it especially hard to change life-styles. Do you? What are the changes you have made in your own life-style in the past year or so?

Perhaps you have cut out the purchase of "junk" foods. One family has reported better health and loss of extra pounds since they quit getting the foods they decided were unnecessary —chips and dips, carbonated drinks, prepared sweet rolls, and desserts. They are enjoying more fresh fruits and vegetables—and liking the change they have made.

Perhaps you have traded cars and bought a small car that gets more mileage. You may have eliminated long trips, tried to visit the interesting places in your own state rather than plan long trips across country or to other countries.

One family we know moved to the country, deciding that the long ride into town was not too big a price to pay for the pleasure of gardening, having more space for four growing children, raising goats, and paying fewer taxes.

One family has decided to invest in art objects, silver, and antiques rather than company stocks which are unpredictable investments.

Low income families are hardest hit. They have little margin for making choices in cost cutting. They already use economy cars or public transportation. A larger proportion of their budget already goes for food and shelter. They have been buying clothes at next-to-new shops for years.

No matter what our income level, we all are affected by the economy. Whatever psychological transitions we may be experiencing at the same time can only enhance the sense of uneasiness and tension we are learning to live with.

Delayed Identity Crisis

Many of us during the middle years are experiencing what one may call a "delayed identity crisis." Both men and women may be going through this sort of gentle transition, but in different ways.

Until the women's movement of the late sixties and early seventies, many people had never questioned the almost total identification of women with the family and men with vocations. For either sex, the person who stepped outside this traditional socialization was regarded as different.

Many women today have happily found their purpose in life by being the best wife and mother they know how. They find fulfillment by being a homemaker.

Many men also believe a man's job is to be the sole provider for the family. Many believe they do not have to concern themselves too much with nurturing the children or management of the home. They feel that if they earn money, pay for a home, make enough to pay for good cars and vacations, camps and college for the children, that ends their responsibility.

This separation of roles for men and women has been the thrust of social, religious, and educational conditioning—as well as the pressure of television advertising.

But for many people in their middle years this traditional sex role conditioning is being questioned. They are asking: Do I have a *being* apart from the stereotyped roles I have accepted? Do I have personality needs and character needs and ability needs that are not satisfied by my spouse and children?

Both women and men find that it is threatening to rethink their identity. But some have started to ask themselves:

- What was I like in my teens?
- What sports did I enjoy?
- What were my outstanding characteristics in school?
- What were the subjects that turned me on?
- In my neighborhood and family, was there anything I was recognized for?
- Did I continue to develop my interests and talents?
- What talent or interest do I wish I had continued?

One good exercise is to think of three characteristics you had when you were in your teens and write them down. These should be adjectives that describe you in some way. One woman recently told me her daughter came home after doing such an exercise at school and shared words she had listed for herself: *athletic, studious, intelligent.*

The mother said, "I would never have dared characterize myself like that. I grew up in the fifties when the emphasis was on a girl being *feminine.* Certainly not athletic or intelligent!"

Men have also been encouraged to develop in certain ways. Even if they had tendencies to be concerned with human relations, with serving, with domestic life, they were required to respond to the Masculine Mystique: Be a football player. Be an athlete. Go into a field where you can make money.

Thus many of us in the middle years are discovering some of the abilities, talents, or interests that we submerged for many years.

Some men have discovered the kitchen. They bake bread or do a gourmet job of barbecuing various meats. Not only are they encouraged to go fishing or hunting, but now they are learning how to fry the fish and roast the venison. My husband, for instance, likes to make jelly. He has enough self confidence to brag about it and to give away jars of jelly for gifts.

Some women are finding they can achieve in areas that were previously regarded the domain of men. They may be financial wizards and have only recently discovered how to put the talent to use in investments or a part-time job. Some women are going into professions previously taboo for women such as medicine, law, and dentistry. Some are competing in athletics although for years they avoided sports.

Whatever our aptitudes were in the childhood and adolescent years, the middle years now presents a new freedom of choice as well as a potential willingness to reject many stereotypes about people.

Forced into Change

Some situations are dropped in our laps. Consider two of the most frightening to us today:

1. the loss of husband or wife;

2. the loss of a job after many years.

There are many more widows than widowers. The life expectancy of women is 75 and the life expectancy of men is 67.5. The chances that a wife will out-live her husband are great. Many women have not even thought about the possibility, much less made any plans for coping with life in that emergency.

In *Widow: The Personal Crisis of a Widow in America*, Lynn Caine points out that the word "widow" has negative connotations. One of every six women over the age of twenty-one's a widow. Not only is the experience a shock, a rude awakening, but the woman so bereft becomes aware of how our society treats a person in this situation.

"Widow" comes from the Sanskrit and it means empty. In the newsroom there is a bit of labeling which suggests the position of a widow. The caption under a photograph may often have an unfinished line, a line which is dangling. This part of the caption is known in journalese as a "widow"— that is, left over.

The widow is regarded as the leftover extension of her husband. Obviously, for a woman who has never defined herself in terms other than as a relative of her husband, this experience is shattering, personal, devastating.

The movie "Alice Doesn't Live Here Any More" is a lively illustration of the delayed identity syndrome.

Alice had been a devoted wife and mother, married to a man who seems selfish and indifferent. She hovers over the dinner until he signals his approval of her cooking. The way they relate to their twelve-year-old son is full of conflict.

When the husband is killed in a truck accident, Alice (Ellen Burstyn) is *thrown into freedom* much against her will. But she has stamina. She has the courage to try to do the only thing she had ever done as a job—singing in a café or night club. Even though she is a mediocre singer, she is persistent, practicing, deciding to move to other places to get singing jobs. Even when she becomes involved with a man who is vicious and violent, she strikes out bravely for the next town, the next job.

Although the picture offers too pat an ending when Kris Kristofferson appears to be her shining rescuer, the film displays the inner/outer struggle one woman faced when confronted with forced freedom. She had forgotten she had a self aside from being a wife.

Divorce or widowhood may strike either men or women. It is a possibility which we should think about.

What of the person who has suddenly lost a job? To be hit with joblessness in the middle years can be the very time when the most responsibilities are weighing you down. In a family where more than one person receives a pay check the trauma may not be so great. Or, one person can train for another job, get additional education while the other is breadwinner.

Women should be encouraged to keep their skills updated with part-time or seasonal work. Some have worked for a couple of years in between having children. Others have developed crafts or vocations that can be pursued while performing domestic duties.

Many families have had to move to a small place, travel to another location to look for jobs, move in with relatives, cut down on the extras of living such as entertainment, pleasure, hobbies, and sports.

Multiple Crises

The possibility of experiencing several difficult situations at once is increased for those of us in the middle years.

One family experienced the breakup of a daughter's marriage at the same time they were going through financial difficulties.

A single middle-aged woman managed the funeral arrangements for her father the same week she was promoted to divisional head in her business office.

A man in his forties tells of changing his career at the same time his grown daughters were moving out, one traveling in Europe, the other undecided as to her own job choice. This man who had been a parish pastor for twenty years said, "I went through a goal reorientation. My goals weren't realistic. I was caught in a trap, caught in the mystique of the parish ministry. For years I had not felt comfortable with it. But I was intimidated by the mystique that the congregation and other pastors in my denomination feel. This mystique of the parish ministry says that it is the highest calling a person can have."

Middle age provides the freedom to say you don't want to be caught in this trap. Having his daughters grown and not needing financial support was one of the liberating factors in his situation. Also, his wife had a responsible job as a librarian which freed him to go into the study of social work.

"I took a career assessment program which told me what I had felt at gut level for several years." He not only found he was qualified for social work but also for ministry. So by pursuing social work studies he increased his options when he finally applied for several jobs.

What was the intimidation he felt? "Persons would wonder why a successful man wanted to give up what he was doing. I received sympathy letters, people saying they were praying for me, sorry to hear I was going through a deep depression. This sort of thing was a typical reaction. It intensifies the struggles when a person is trying to find a new direction." People find it hard to appreciate the process of struggle that another person is experiencing if they are not experiencing it too."

The same is true of women who are satisfied with their own choices—either the domestic life, a career, or a combination of the two. It is hard to make room in our heads for more than one kind of image.

Emerging Roles for Women and Men

Working out one's identity may be a life long process. Some

persons find themselves, so to speak, early in life, building on their self discovery as the years pass.

Others, like Grandma Moses, come to their last decades before they discover the creativity never before allowed to emerge.

A good book to examine is *Emerging Roles for Women and Men* by Carol and Conrad W. Weiser, edited by Mary Whitten and Raymond Tiemeyer. It is a program for people who are interested in new interpretations of old roles. For instance:

"Married women wonder whether their homes and families are limiting them. Women who are employed question why their positions are controlled rather than controlling. Professional women resent the acute lags in their salaries when compared to those of their male counterparts.

"At the same time, some men are becoming aware that certain traditions confine them to sex roles which do not match their interests or use their qualifications. They would like to see more freedom to be what they wish, but find social pressures unyielding.

"Still other men and women are uncomfortable with the change in role identity. They do not understand the change or the reasons behind it, and so are afraid of it."

This book provides an opportunity for women and men to examine the issues in the light of Christian theology and belief. Through the use of role play, mini-posters and analysis of Scripture, people can identify their own interests and roles and work out more constructive attitudes.

The authors point out that some people may begin to feel guilty because they have lived the way they were expected to live decades ago. A woman may think she is being taught now that she should have pursued a career rather than become a homemaker. If so she may feel guilty and angry. A man may feel that he is now being cast in the role of oppressor, whereas society formerly required him to assume complete economic and social responsibility for his family. He may become resentful. Both people were taught certain moral obligations. Now it seems as if these earlier moral obligations were unnecessary. Because needs and conditions change, what was generally acceptable yesterday may be unacceptable to many people today.

So, who are we? Is "identity crisis" a fair phrase to describe our generation? I think what we see is a variety of moods and directional changes. We are pressured and pulled by many forces. We see possibilities for our lives, on the one hand, and yet we feel trapped, on the other. We want to consider our own needs, but obviously we must consider the needs of those closest to us. However, whether identity crisis or not, this can be a time of fantastic opportunity.

We need to learn to see the new images and meanings bubbling in this exciting time, to be real, alive, whole, human, willing to launch out on our own, perhaps coming into conflict with the needs and desires of persons close to us. We should risk being "me."

In essence our identity is to be free—free from unrealistic expectations, free to stop hiding behind the responsibilities we have to others so that we can learn how to measure opportunity, or how to respond to it, when it comes.

The middle years can be a time of moving out of shadows of old images that may be repressing us and restricting our potential. A time to view a possible world of trouble and conflict, as a world of opportunity.

Here is our challenge: to share the feelings and insecurities of the middle years with other women and men who may feel as frustrated and puzzled as we sometimes do. It is a chance to pause, take stock of who we are and what we want to be, and to look ahead to make the whole of our life count for the most.

3.

Who Do You Talk To?

RACHEL CONRAD WAHLBERG

Ideally, the middle years should reflect a growing expertise in the art of communication. We've had years to practice, to learn from our successes and failures. On the other hand, those years may have resulted in many destructive communication patterns becoming habitual. So, let's take a fresh look at this often neglected subject.

Everyone, not just those in mid-life, is bombarded with communication from all sides:

- billboards shout at us from the roadside;
- announcers on radio give us news, music, commercials;
- newspapers and magazines litter our tables and family rooms;
- family members tell us what's happening in their lives;
- people at work, school, or the supermarket add their comments.

We've been living in a sea of communication. Often we are so overwhelmed that we find it difficult to sort out whom we want to listen to, who we want to talk with, what we think about what we hear.

People begin, change, and end relationships by talking with

one another. Communication is their channel of influence. One author in the field of public relations claims that people spend about 70 percent of their waking hours in some form of communication—talking and listening, reading and writing, sharing in some way with other human beings.

If I say something to you, first of all I had to think about it in my own head. Someone has said that life is nothing more than a rush of thoughts inside the head. Some are kept inside —and we regard that as thinking. Some thoughts we express to other people. We regard that as talk or conversation. Some talk we write down on paper. We compose, make formal our speech, our thoughts take form in an orderly way. That is writing or literature, news, poetry, etc.

Basically we build on what is inside our mental processes. We know that we think about a variety of things, that our minds are functioning most of the time. Sometimes when we want to rest we cannot because we can't turn our minds off. Especially if we have been upset, or have been to an exciting event, a play, film, or seen a dramatic television program.

We receive input from many sources—our reading, watching TV, studying, visiting, hearing other people talk, listening to the radio. In this way our minds are stimulated by the minds and happenings about us.

A person, then, is not only a body but an ongoing conversation in the head. A person relates to other people by establishing contact and trying to communicate the ideas in her or his mind to that other person, trusting that the other person will have understandings of the words used that will make clear the meanings the speaker intended.

This factor is important to communication—that the words or symbols used by one person be also understood in the same way by the other person. If we come from similar backgrounds and cultures, our understandings are probably similar. If we come from different cultures, our understandings are not the same.

Communication and the Family

Recently I visited my father who is eighty years old. Since he became widowed two years ago, he talks aloud to himself in his small house. He is thinking out loud many of the thoughts he used to share with his wife of fifty-four years. This practice does not embarrass him or his family and friends. They understand his need to express himself. As he puts it, "I like conversation with an intelligent person."

As a retired pastor, he studies for the children's catechism class he teaches. He is currently supplying the church in a small community. He thinks out loud about his sermon outlines and even practices parts of his sermon as an actor goes over a part. In this way his thoughts and arguments flow through his mental processes. Talking is a way of life.

The family is the first place we learn to communicate. The home is a teacher. We learn our first words there. We learn to respond to the speech of others. We learn to identify others. The baby learns to respond to family members by naming the persons. The response to another person means a recognition of the other person's existence. The parent has reality for the child.

The small child learns to mimic the speech in the home. Whatever the language of the culture, of the surrounding family, that is the language the child learns.

The family is the most exciting of all small groups. It is a microcosm of the world. Here there is intimacy and formality. Here there is rivalry and love. Here there is openness and shutness. Here there is building up and tearing down.

Here there are opportunities to learn and share, to be separate and distant, to be angry, to be selfish. The family is the chief learning center for each child for several years, until school or peer groups take over.

Talking is based upon relationships. The relationships within the family change from day to day and year to year. They change between the time of marriage and the arrival of the first child. They change between the time of the first child and later children. Relationships may subtly change when there is a crisis in the family, when the family reacts to prosperity or trouble.

Relationships can change from oneness to estrangement, from forgiveness to greater awareness of each other as persons. Or from hate to rejection. Or from love to hate.

A recent film by Ingmar Bergman, "Scenes from a Marriage," shows how a relationship can disintegrate and years later come to a partial reconciliation. A married couple are vividly portrayed in the first scenes as if they conceive of themselves as an ideal couple.

Posing for pictures for a national magazine, the woman and the man do not recognize their frustrations and the games they are playing. In small ways they put each other down, and fail to recognize each other as full persons. Their marriage has fallen into destructive patterns. Each is still trying to be what the other expected and what their parents expected. They are also playing an "I'm OK—You're OK" game which can only lead to unhappiness.

It is not until they separate, divorce, and marry other persons, that they come to see each other as full persons with needs of his/her own. Their attitudes change, and to a degree, the way they relate to each other. Bergman does not offer a neat ending, but the film is provocative, effective in its effort to show the uneven path of one relationship over a period of years.

Who Do You Talk to in Your Home?

It is not true that we communicate to each person in a family in the same way. The lines of communication are of varying kinds. We may have different attitudes toward each child. We may be critical of one child, admire the child who has some of our own traits, or lean toward the child who is most affectionate toward us.

We may try to force on a child a skill we wanted in childhood, not realizing the verbal pressure involved. Once a father was heard to say of his ten-year-old son after visiting the fifth grade football practice: "He's not aggressive enough. He won't get out there and fight!" Apparently the father wanted his son to develop into a skilled athlete whether or not it was consistent with the boy's wishes or abilities. He may have felt an athletic inadequacy when he himself was a youth.

We, who are parents, without knowing it, may show different faces to different children. To the oldest we may communicate a stern and rigid set of rules. They reflect an anxious concern to be good parents. To another, younger child, we may act more relaxed, may be more concerned to understand the child's ideas, wishes, and listen to his or her objections to rules and expectations.

Think of *how you are* with each person in the home. Ask yourself: am I warm? critical? affirming? easily angry? impatient? unlistening?

By the middle years we have very skillfully learned to communicate with different styles in different environments. In a gathering of friendly people we act one way—we are relaxed and talkative. We feel at home with them. In business we may present a serious-minded façade, careful to appear as knowing our business, careful not to expose ourselves to mockery or criticism.

In a church group where we are well known, we may show our "good side," try to be exemplars of community standards, sound, upright, and "Christian." Among relatives we may revert to childish antagonisms felt years ago with brothers and sisters. And among in-laws we may attempt cordiality or a certain reserve, hoping to please the spouse's family, holding in mind the many things we know about that family background.

To each other as adult friends or as wife and husband, we communicate in still another way. In public we may act like strangers to one another. Among friends, affectionate. In the kitchen, indifferent, each doing cooking or chores. And in the bedroom, frank and intimate. The reverse, affectionate in public and cold in intimate situations, is also a widespread married life-style.

We notice, too, that our children have different responses to each other and to us as parents. One boy can't stand his sister. A big brother or sister may boss the younger ones. Sisters and brothers several years apart may move in such different worlds that they hardly notice one another, whereas two who are close may share confidences and be friends for many years.

There are no two relationships in a family which are the same. We have heard people say, "I treat them all alike." Of course this is impossible. Each parent has a separate relationship with each child; each child a separate relationship with each parent.

In one family a strong wife-husband relationship may be at the center. Imagine a line reaching out to each child and then a line reaching between each two people, criss-crossing until each person has a line to each other person.

If you, for instance, have three children, how many relationships have you in your home? That means in a family of five, there are twenty relationships. There's ongoing conversation in all these criss-cross directions.

Or think of a home where there is one parent. The parent may support the family financially as well as tending to their daily needs. This single parent may have a strong relationship with one child on whom she/he relies, and perhaps a "pet" relationship with the youngest family member. Other children may hold responsibilities in the home, learning to cope earlier than children with two parents.

Remembering the family in which you grew up, imagine a diagram of its relationships. Between which individuals were the strong lines of communication? Which child got along best with your parents? Did you feel closer to one parent? Did you feel put upon, with too many chores? Or more like a functional member with privileges and responsibilities?

Today, in your own home, where are the strong lines of communication? With which person do you feel freest to talk about what is on your mind? To which person do you show the most sympathy, are you most eager to support with comfort and encouragement? Which person is most non-communicative?

If your children are already adult and living in the community, how much contact do you have? Do you have an informal pattern of phoning or dropping in? Or do you keep a distance because that is what the young adult seems to prefer?

If you are a single person, with whom do you communicate from your original family? In this community do you share a daily visit with friends, or do you rely on your work to provide ongoing relationships? Do you have a few people you can call on when you need to talk? Or do you find loneliness a real problem?

Two people may talk a great deal, or be silent for hours at a time. They can be communicating even when not talking. They can feel a closeness, a sharing, a presence.

Two people can think of their relationship as an ongoing conversation between them. When a person loses a marriage partner of many long years, the greatest shock seems to be losing the companionship of that person. The response from that human being was something they could count on. Lady Bird Johnson wrote after her husband's death that she often thought, "I'll tell Lyndon about that." Or she would turn down a page of a book as she always had, intending to read him a passage.

Consider all the ways people communicate in a marriage:

- living together;
- sharing plans, cooking, household chores;
- having children, raising them and constantly discussing them;
- going places together: social events, church, vacations;
- having problems and working through them;

- having pleasures and reflecting on them;
- sharing affection and sexual intimacy;
- sharing home base as they look out on the community and nation, the church, and other institutions, commenting and growing as they share.

Every aspect of the relationship has a part in communication. Just talking over the events of the day gives warmth and a binding element to the marriage.

This is the magic of communication—there's more to it than meets the ear. More than the words are the feelings under the words, the images called up in the mind, the vibrations that the other person feels about the one who is talking or listening.

"Experiencing the other side" is Martin Buber's phrase for describing true dialogue. Reuel Howe says that it means to feel an event from the side of the person one meets as well as from one's own side.

And then a mysterious thing happens. As we know another person, and are known by her/him, we know ourselves more deeply. We absorb what others feed into us—as we listen to the happenings inside them. We react out of our depths or lifelong experience. It all adds up to a broader experience of living, of sharing one's depths with another human being.

Herein is God in our lives. Luther included communication between human beings as a sacrament. God moves in our lives as we become closer to one another, moving in our spirits as we become more fully human and more fully God's creatures on earth.

Ways of Communication

You speak in many ways to people. Perhaps you offer direct comments and advice. When a person opens up with, "I don't know what to do. What would you do?" it may offer you some options. You encourage the person to consider the possibilities as you see them. Maybe you tell the person what you did in a similar situation.

Shared interest. Another way you communicate with a person is through sharing a common interest. People who love sports, gardening, or health foods, get a conversation going with no trouble at all. People who like controversial political questions, can get right into current national problems on what they see as a political crisis, and find a common ground for discussion. If you share an interest with your intimate friends or a child, you share a world. You have a common language or vocabulary, a common outlook perhaps, an excitement about doing and learning in this area.

Responsibilities. Since we communicate through our work, in our homes we are likely to share some responsibilities. How work is spread around among family members communicates ideas about power, importance, and sex roles.

Usually we try to teach small children responsibilities commensurate with their age level. To make a bed, to set the table, clean the bathtub, pick up his/her possessions—all are jobs that children can do. For one parent to be the "pick-up person" of the family gives the child a certain message. It says: you can always expect adults, especially a mommy or daddy to pick up after you. A recent *Sunday Weekly* magazine reported this incident:

A teacher had been teaching her class about magnets. The children had examined magnets and practiced using them. When the teacher asked on a quiz, "What is a six-letter word starting with "m" that picks up things?" all the children wrote down, "mother."

If the child is expected to learn to be self sufficient and independent by being allowed and encouraged to tend to personal needs, he or she gets the message: You are smart enough to do these things for yourself. It is part of growing up to learn to wait on yourself and to cooperate in the family.

Sometimes it is not until the middle years that a wife and husband reassess the jobs in the home. They were so used to the work divisions when the children were small that they fail to see they can become less rigidly scheduled. Some couples have talked over their job assignments and become more independent in tending to their own needs. Perhaps other aspects of sharing have entered in. The wife may have an outside job—so both share in the operation of the home. There may be less money—or more money—which makes a difference.

Values Sharing. As the years have passed, we have absorbed values from the surrounding culture, from our own family experiences, from our neighbors. Often we don't think about what we are implying when we say wistfully, "I wish I had a boat and a cabin at the lake." "I wish I had a Mercedes-Benz." "I wish I could sit around and play bridge."

When we say, "We plan to vote for so and so in the city election," the guest or neighbor knows that civic responsibility is taken seriously. When we say to a guest, "We go to church at ten o'clock on Sunday," the guest knows what to expect.

Parental Choice. We make choices for children—and sometimes we make choices for each other. Perhaps we wanted a child to study piano, take art lessons, play football. We may have imposed the lessons or encouraged the child in that field. We set an example of going to church and other congregational activities, thus saying to our children that we consider these activities important.

Sometimes we pressure the other adult in the home to buy something, go somewhere, not to do something, etc. Here again, our values are being displayed. One man says, "My wife won't let me go to that restaurant without a coat." What he means is that his wife wishes he would wear one, and may threaten not to go with him if he doesn't dress "properly." In another home such a matter would not be an issue at all.

Messages on television, on blackboards and billboards are no more vivid than our everyday expressions of our likes, wishes, and comments about what others do.

Silence. Another means of communication is our silence. Sometimes we show offense, hostility, or disappointment by being silent toward another person. This is not hard to read, to hear . . . to feel. We get negative vibrations from the other person's aloofness.

We can use silence another way. If we never discuss current political events in the nation and in the world, never read the news or turn on a newscast, what does this say to others around us?

—We may not be interested.

—We feel ignorant and don't want to show it.

—We are so involved in other things we do not have time for daily news and politics.

Anyone of us who reads magazines and newspapers, and listens to television has ideas about current events. We have ideas about differences in religion, about work and pleasure, about food and drink, about hair styles.

Chances are we talk to those around us about the things we are vitally concerned with. If it's the neighbors, we talk, and if it's religion, we talk. If it's movies or fashion or city politics, we can usually find some listeners who will respond to us. If it's a local scandal, it's even easier.

If we are silent about certain areas, it may mean only that we do not feel interested or articulate in that area.

For example, we may seldom speak about our faith, what Jesus means to us, what prayer has meant in our lives. We may never open the Scriptures or go to church. On the other hand, we may go fairly regularly and still not be able to express ourselves.

Something of what we think and feel is conveyed by our silence or our attention.

Overcoming Conflicts in Communicating

Because we spend so much of our day communicating, we think we understand what is going on—what it's all about.

There is an explosion of communications today—all sorts of media. Constantly we hear news, read books, and magazines. We can't eat dinner until we hear the news or go to bed until we have heard the late edition of the same news. We search the TV guide for programs to identify with.

It is not only words that convey meaning but the raised eyebrow, the put-down tone, the shaken finger, the whistle, the smile, the winked eye.

Thus there are sights, sounds, and sensations which all feed into what we hear and understand about what's going on in our world.

We think we understand words since we hear them all the time. But sometimes there is much more to the words than a simple meaning.

Words, as we know, are symbols. They can be symbols for such things as breakfast, table, car, home. They can be symbols for abstract ideas such as love, hate, anger, frustration, tiredness. We understand that to use the word *love* is not the emotion itself. It merely suggests to your mind and my mind that we are talking about feelings, the way one person feels about another. We both have to understand what we are talking about. That is, to communicate effectively the sender's words must mean the same thing to the receiver that they do to the sender.

The word communication is derived from the Latin *communis*, meaning "common." What we are doing when we communicate is to establish a commonness.

Our need is in common with the needs of others. As Agnes de Mille put it, "We all want an encounter with an awakened mind." Popular songs have suggested that there are personal needs to be met: "You and Me against the World," or "Free to Be You and Me."

Here's a problem to illustrate. Perhaps a husband wants to tell his wife, or a wife her husband, to be more approving. She or he may think of it in these terms:

- My husband/wife never tells me anything affirmative.
- I would like to be complimented once in a while.
- I always feel he or she is going to criticize me for something I've done.

- I wish he or she would give me verbal "strokes."
- I need to be built up, not put down.
- The things I do—my talents, the activities I engage in for the family, my work—are never praised. They are taken for granted. My performance each day is as if it doesn't happen. Only little things are complained about.

Now, if you were that needing person, how would you get across what you want to communicate?

First, try to understand the other person's position. Whatever you see will come through to her or him through the desires, needs, perceptions, and expectations that person already has.

In other words, you know that what you are about to suggest is also a real idea, perhaps a need in the other person's life. If you can relate your need to her or his need, there will be understanding.

For instance, you could say at some moment when you have praised something the other person has done, "I give you a boost, why don't you try to give me a boost now and then?" Or, to avoid putting the other person on the defensive: "I, too, need to be built up and approved."

By this process you have done three things:

1. You have related to her or his need for approval and affirmation in a positive way.
2. You have made a suggestion about your own desire or need in a similar area.
3. Therefore, you have created awareness, consideration of a person/need and made yourself vulnerable or open to the other person.

You have sought out a change in the other person, but one that is compatible with what he or she understands in his/her own life.

The Process of Change

Herbert F. Lionberger reports these five steps in the adoption of an idea, practice, or change:

1. Awareness—you learn about the idea of practice.
2. Interest—you are stimulated to have an interest in it.
3. Evaluation—you try it out mentally, think about it.
4. Trial—you use it a time or two as an experiment.
5. Adoption—you adopt it as a pattern or for full scale use.

Thus, to follow the example: If we are *made aware* of our spouse's need for affirmation we may proceed to the second step because we are *interested* in what the partner desires. The partner then *evaluates* the idea for change, thinking about what he or she could praise the other person for.

Then a tentative *try* at accommodation would be next.

"I really admire your persistence in your job. You are really a good dad to the children. You manage the home well. You are so much fun to be around. I didn't know you could do that so well!"

If this effort is met with appreciation, the pattern of affirmation or "strokes" may then become a pattern which will enhance the relationship.

In similar ways we change our ideas about a controversial issue—equal rights for women or minorities, abortion, detente with Russia or China—or whether our congregation should change something in its worship practice.

To achieve cooperation from the people we want to influence or change, we must understand where they are in their own thinking and feelings in order to create awareness.

If you are emotionally involved in the position you hold, the harder it is to change that position. To be committed to an idea, belief, or practice means that the very commitment itself becomes a barrier to change. According to Cutlip and Center, people who are less interested in a matter are easier to change or influence.

For instance, if paving streets on the other side of town is the question before the city council, you could easily be unconcerned. It is not your street. You are not emotionally involved.

But if the city council wants to put up a building in your neighborhood which will increase traffic, endanger the safety of your children, and cut off the view you have from your house, then you become emotionally involved.

Let's say, for example, that your congregation is going to introduce girl acolytes when only boys have been performing this service. If you have no children in this age level you may not be concerned. But if your son enjoys being acolyte and his turn will be reduced from every other Sunday to once every three months, you may put up resistance because your child is affected.

Awareness is the first stage of concern about an issue. We are most influenced here by the news media. What we read in newspapers, magazines, and books, what we see on television, what we hear on the radio—these are tremendous influences in our becoming aware of issues, and in the next stage of growing interest.

But when it comes to mental consideration of an idea, we are inclined to lean more on our friends, families, and neighbors for discussion about the issue. If it's a political issue, a conflict in the news, or a national problem it is vitally important to talk it over with others in our intimate circle:

- closest friend and/or marriage partner;
- family members, including children;
- social group and neighbors;
- people at work or at church.

There is a need for reinforcement, a need to talk things over with people who are important in our life.

We also turn to support groups, such as civic clubs, social organizations, church groups. People whom we respect in these groups may have different ideas or experiences. And even though we may not agree with them, if we are developing our own thinking about a subject, it is helpful to know what the other person thinks and how she or he reacts to the subject. The other person's life experience may help in our mental/emotional/spiritual growth.

To communicate is to live with others in a verbal, articulating sense. But it also means to share with others our life experience on many levels—nonverbal, emotional, work activities, community concern, and the broad impact and conditioning we share as being part of the same culture.

God Talk Is Communication

There is a turning-toward-God that is the undergirding of our lives if we are Christian. We don't just say formal prayers. We don't wait for Sunday to participate in what we call corporate worship. We have an ongoing relationship with God as we have ongoing relationships with friends and family.

The difference is that it is an inner relationship, a reliance on spiritual guidance and communication.

We may feel that our whole lives are a turning in the direction of God, or a reliance on a Jesus-awareness to guide us as we go through the day. (See chapter 8 on living "in Christ" and what this means.)

Jesus emphasized not only an acceptance of persons without stereotyping them, but he put down the Pharisees who lived through a false emphasis on rules and regulations. They had made the law into an impersonal system.

We can become too preoccupied with our own moral state—always taking our spiritual temperature and checking ourselves to see if our brownie points for the day have been earned.

Jesus taught people to look on others as people to care about, to give, to affirm, to help, to forgive—and in so doing, to love one's self.

Jesus was not just a great religious figure, but a Relationship Event. His ministry was based on the way he related to human beings. He affirmed them, drew them out, made them feel God loved and accepted them.

The way Jesus related to people can be a pattern for our own life of *talking, hearing, listening, seeing, and sharing* in the middle years.

4.

Who Do You Care About?

RACHEL CONRAD WAHLBERG

Some people are going to like me and some people aren't, so I might as well be me. Then at least I will know that the people who like me, like me.
                                         Hugh Prather

Some years ago a retreat leader asked a group of adults who they wanted to be like. I was one of the participants and the question struck me as one big blank. As people went around the room giving their answers I felt embarrassed. I could not think of anyone I used as a model or wanted "to be like." I said with a shrug, "I just want to be me—develop all the potential in *me.*"

Everyone else had a model to suggest . . . a parent or a teacher, a well known celebrity . . . a great figure in the past. Somehow I felt embarrassed for having said what I said about being "me."

One of Jesus' sayings which would receive a high vote for the most ignored part of Scripture, is his admonition to "love your neighbor *as yourself.*" We have heard a great deal about loving one's neighbor—but almost nothing in traditional Christian instruction about *loving ourselves.*

Be a servant. Deny yourself. Give to others. Consider others. Submerge your own interests to serve the Lord. Minister to others. All of this, yes.

But *love* yourself? This sounds like heresy. Think for a moment about being made in the image of God.

We are going to consider in this chapter the people we care about. We are going to take this Jesus phrase seriously, the idea that we love our neighbors as ourselves. It is a directive.

Think of a concentric circle.

Beyond *self*, we reach out to *others*: to our brothers and sisters; to our own parents; to our children at home and our adult children elsewhere; to our friends and acquaintances; the people next door.

To the people in our community and nation. Not just in our own economic and educational class, but in others, at the supermarket, at the cafeteria.

To people of other denominations and other faiths.

To people of the world . . . the affluent people as well as the starving people of Africa, India, and Pakistan.

What is our responsibility to ourselves and to others on this broad scale?

One of the most popular books in recent years has been Thomas Harris' *I'm OK—You're OK*. People have latched onto it because they search for assurance that they are acceptable, that deep down in their own beings there is some worth, so that they don't always have to be proving themselves. People want to learn that they don't have to build themselves up by putting someone else down.

As Harris points out, we don't have to be always pleasing the parent tape imbedded in our memory. We don't have to be pleasing or impressing the other persons around us. We can relax, accept them and accept ourselves.

A Judgmental Christianity

Unfortunately Christianity has been identified in many times and places as a judgmental religion. It placed more emphasis on judgment and damnation than on self acceptance, being made in the image of God, and the forgiveness and redemption provided through Jesus' life, death, and resurrection.

A year ago our daughter was involved with a religious group which seemed to encourage anxiety and a judgmental spirit. After the first few weeks, she seemed oppressed by her new faith. During a summer vacation in which she was not able to get a job, she read her Bible much of the time, listened to radio preachers, and was concerned about "being ready."

Reading newspapers, magazines, and watching television were "of the devil," she told us. She had been "saved" she said, but seemed uptight about this new experience.

"Are you saved?" she asked me. "Of course, all Christians are saved who believe in Jesus," I answered. Did I remember a day when the Holy Spirit came over me? "No, not everyone," I pointed out, "has to have a Damascus experience like Paul did. Many people who have grown up in the church feel they have believed all their lives."

She spoke of being led to "witness" to people who were "living by the devil." She could tell who they are, she said. "Then you would be God," I objected. "It is not up to you to decide who is 'of the devil' and who is 'of God.'"

When she claimed that God was giving her this power, my response was, "No, that is for God alone to judge. You can witness to people without judging them as being 'of the devil' or 'of the Spirit.'"

Our daughter was extremely anxious about the Second Coming. She had to be ready. When we told her the early Christians were also convinced it was imminent in their own generation and were wrong, she was not impressed. As parents we were concerned that this new religious experience caused anxiety rather than peace and self acceptance.

As the summer wore on and she got several weeks of part-time work, she seemed less intense. As she got ready to go back to college, she became less pressured and oppressed by her church experience.

Unfortunately, it was this sort of Pharisaic judgmental

attitude that caused some of the saddest chapters in the history of Christendom. Wars and crusades were based on the principle: if you don't see the issues just as we righteous people see them, then you must be heretics and infidels.

Jesus was critical of the Pharisees who set up strict rules and regulations for themselves and judged other people by their own strict standards—and who inconsistently practiced a life lacking in love and compassion.

Even people such as Luther and Calvin were influential in causing the persecution of people who did not believe as they did. Although Martin Luther deplored the extremes that some of his followers went to in the Peasants' Rebellion, he helped stimulate their rebellion and later urged the nobles to destroy the uprising. Calvin caused the burning at the stake of a man named Servetus because of his interpretation of an article of faith.

How could Christian "love" lead to persecution? A good book to read on the Reformers handling of this and other knotty problems is Charles Anderson's, *The Reformation— Then and Now*. Even before the Reformation, the Inquisition had been established as an aid in the fight against heresy. Simply put, says Anderson, "the Inquisition was a device to search out heresy and then to correct or destroy it. It was reasoned that it is far better for one to suffer for a short while now in order to be corrected, than to suffer eternally because of some false religious notion."

Coming from this sort of judgmental history, and the more recent American experience of puritanism and pietism, it has been quite difficult for many Christians to learn to emphasize the love and acceptance they find in Jesus and the Christian message.

It is no wonder that *to love others* has been emphasized at the expense of loving *one's self*.

How Do You Love Yourself?

It is a fascinating assignment to ask yourself: in what ways do I love myself?

We care about our bodies. We live inside a physical body. We are sexual human beings. We look out on the world through eyes, ears and skin sensitivity. We smell, we taste, we like, we dislike. We try to take care of our bodies through daily care and nourishment. Maybe we aren't consistent but we try to show concern for our bodies in many ways:

Eating nutritious foods. We try to select foods we enjoy among those we know are "good for us." We indulge ourselves in some food and drink that may not be good for us. Unless we are burdened with anxieties we avoid destructive patterns of overeating, overdrinking, smoking, etc.

Taking physical care of our needs. We try to get exercise, preferably in ways we enjoy.

Taking care of health problems as they arise. We have annual checkups, reporting ailments to the doctor, seeking health advice from professionals.

We care about our minds. In *The Bridge of San Luis Rey* Thornton Wilder described a woman like this: "All her existence lay in the burning center of her mind."

We don't think much about it, but we live our lives as an ongoing rush of thoughts through our mental processes. We may be inclined to take mental activity for granted. Once we have made it through school, we may feel inclined to consider ourselves educated. If we are intellectually curious, however, we may pursue a life long process of continuing education—through reading, study, writing, sharing conversation and discussion with family and small groups, perhaps taking courses at different times in our lives.

We practice some selectivity in the television we watch, turning off the meaningless nonsense programs that bore us to death. We select the movies we go to see, the periodicals we subscribe to. We may be inclined to pick up a good magazine rather than watch a mediocre program someone else is watching on TV.

We care about our relationships with others. Later we shall consider the wide range of these relationships, but this interpersonal care is an aspect of our self love. It is important to us how people respond to us. We want to be seen in a good light by others—our family, our friends, people at the job, people in our church and other organizations.

We care about our life planning. Some of us are thinking ahead to the time when we retire. Are we saving, buying property, making contacts that have to do with our retirement years? Or do we like to keep busy so much that we think in terms of our hobbies, sports, and other interests which we could expand into jobs in later years?

In the past when we made work/vocation choices we considered our preferences as well as our abilities. And now, as we get older, we may be concerned more than ever with what pleases us.

We care about our reputation, our image in the public we know. We perform acts, we take care of responsibilities so that we are respected in the community. This gives us ego-satisfaction, makes us proud of ourselves. Sometimes we have a negative self image. It may be caused by the way we've been treated, our lack of experiencing success, a cluster of causes and influences.

Historical Christianity, unfortunately, has encouraged women especially, to have negative self images. Some of the ideas women have internalized are:

- the Eve image
- woman as unclean
- woman as subordinate
- don't touch a woman
- women keep quiet!
- woman can't be a witness

We care about ourselves in a selfish way, too, although it is difficult to admit. We want enough money to live comfortably. We want a few luxuries. And since we grew up in depression times, we might feel especially greedy about some possessions. At the same time we may experience this sort of self indulgence as arousing guilt in our self consciousness, in our psyche. If we were brought up to be self-denying and to serve others, we rationalize our material blessing: That purchase was a bargain: this antique or painting or piece of silver is an investment.

We put the best construction or interpretation on what we do and say. Interpretation is an important part of life. One person may be called an innovator or a genius while another label for the same person may be "radical" or "instigator." Bobby Kennedy's enemies thought him "arrogant" and an "upstart," while his friends considered him "dedicated," "persistent," and "patriotic." Martha Mitchell has been cruelly labeled as outspoken and ridiculous—while her husband, John Mitchell, who admitted that he thought almost anything was justified to get Richard Nixon elected, has had no scathing articles written about him.

It is in this nonjudgmental way we often "put the best face" on what we do. We may even shrug off characteristics in ourselves that we criticize in others. A father complains a child is rebellious and stubborn, never remembering his own youthful rebellions. Thus, we are biased in our favor.

Not only do we look out for our own self interest in these and many other ways, but we enjoy ourselves. How many times have you thought: "I had fun doing that"? Maybe you worked in your garden, spent the afternoon outdoors working on some project, went to play golf, made a speech, wrote a poem, played with a neighbor's child. Maybe a stimulating conversation with friends you took out to dinner gave you such a glow that you felt it was a peak experience.

Maybe you rose to a challenge and did a good job. Yes, you enjoyed it.

One more aspect of loving ourselves is to realize our limitations and accept them. We do not have to do everything and be everything. We don't even have to do anything well. As someone said recently, "If it's worth doing, it's worth doing badly" —that is, we don't have to *do perfectly* everything at hand.

Some people become compulsive trying to do too many

things and trying to do each one of them perfectly. One woman puts up stacks of Christmas boxes tied in neat bows. One man won't permit any family members to work in the garage because they "might mess things up."

Some people neglect their families because they anxiously need to be the top person in their company, or the person who does the most church work, or become the most visible community service person in the neighborhood.

Usually the basis of this spirit of drivenness is a feeling of insecurity, "I can't like myself if I don't do all this work." Another source of our compulsions is that we live in a competitive society. We were brought up to be achievement oriented, so it is very difficult for us to say: "I will relax and do a few things I enjoy and let a few other activities go."

An important facet of faith comes to bear here. In spiritual terms, we do not have to earn our salvation by accumulating brownie points. God loves us as we are. He does not have our American sense of achievement. Indeed, God may rate a kind deed or a relaxed conversation with our spouse or a family friend as worth more than getting a larger paycheck.

The Concentric Circle of Caring

Even if it is hard to admit it, each of us, a *self*, is at the center of concentric circles of caring in our lives. We reach out from our own being to touch and communicate with:

- our own siblings—brothers and sisters
- our parents
- if married, our marriage partner
- our children
- our immediate friends
- our neighbors
- the people we contact in our work
- daily contacts—at the school, the bank, the grocery
- community people
- people we know far away

- vague groups we are concerned about, such as hungry millions in our countries.

A word about being the *center* of all this concern.

Christians especially have been conditioned not to be the center of their lives. And in this sense—a spiritual centering—we recognize that our faith in God through Christ is the center of our lives. But for daily living and showing concern for all whom we care about, we function as the center of our compass, the chief actor on our personal stage, as the fulcrum of our lives.

It is my body that has to get out of bed. It is my personal decision-making that is involved with what to wear, what to eat, what work I do, providing for the family, running errands, planning for the future.

We must not be ashamed or self conscious about functioning from *me as center*.

Of course to care only for ourselves would be conceited, wrong, sinful. But to acknowledge our own beings, created in God's image, as the pivotal point from which we move, work, feel and think, is OK.

Although at the moment we are most closely concerned with the persons living in our house—house mates, marriage partners, children—let us first think back in our lives to family arrangements which preceded the present.

Siblings. Our own brothers and sisters may be far away from us now. Or they may live in the same town or the same state. However, for the first years of our lives, the formative childhood and teen years, we shared everything with them in our parents' household.

As my sister and I have said to each other with some astonishment, "We are the only two women in the world who came out of that childhood in North Carolina with *those* two parents and grandparents, and those three brothers." Although half a continent apart, when we get together we remember and share dozens of tidbits of life, memories, attitudes.

As much as we may not like to admit it, our relations with those family members had a great deal to do with the way we are now. For instance:

Where did you come in the family? Your place in the family structure was crucial to what responsibilities you had, how you responded to your parents, how you related to your sisters and brothers. Some psychologists have ventured to say that birth order determines much of the personality we develop in life.

Were you given lots of responsibility? If you were the oldest of several children—or an only child—you were probably permitted to do things for yourself, perform some tasks in the household that younger children were not allowed.

Were you spoiled and protected? If you were a younger child you may have been the object of everyone's concern. In my family, it was said of the youngest son: "Paul didn't learn to talk for a long time. All he needed to do was grunt and point and everyone jumped to give him what he wanted."

Was there a wide age spread among the children in your family? If so, you may not have been close to any sister or brother. Sometimes an older child "mothers" or "fathers" the younger ones. My mother, who was one of eight children, says she was reared by her older sister who was sixteen years older than she. "I would go to my sister if I had a problem," she said.

Many psychological studies have been done in recent years on family position. There are no hard and fast conclusions, since obviously parents, heritage, and communities are different. But many similarities and/or tendencies exist among those who had a certain position in the family.

What is our relationship today to those sisters and brothers who are now adults? Some families stay quite close, especially if they are in one small community, or if they have grown up with a warm sense of family. Others never see their adult family members until a long vacation trip takes them to another part of the country.

Or we may not see a sister or brother until we meet at the funeral of a close relative. Since the trauma of the funeral is in the foreground this experience can arouse a mixture of emotions.

Keeping in touch with the family can be done in many ways, through phone calls, family letters, and by planning a large family reunion.

Because we care for each other, and because there is a certain cluster of traditions that our family may have, it is a good idea to think about these relationships and how we might enhance communication.

Responsibility to Parents

What about our parents? How do we care for them? What are our responsibilities to them?

A great deal has been written about the decline of the large family and the exclusiveness of the nuclear family.

Since 30 percent of United States people move to another location each year, there is less opportunity for adult children to keep close to parents, and almost no probability that older parents move along with their grown children. Houses are smaller and are not usually constructed for dual families.

Some of us have added on to our homes to accomodate a parent who lives alone. Many of us have parents who still manage quite well by themselves. Some have parents in homes for the aged, rest homes, or who need some sort of daily care.

A new concept just being established is to provide day care for older persons who are alone all day, but who need some sort of assistance. Some church groups and social service groups are setting up "adult day care centers" to serve people in this category.

What is the situation with your own parents? Are they in good health? Do you keep in contact with them, visit them? Are they so far away you have to make a major trip to see them?

Have sisters and brothers had to make any joint decision in case of the parents' illness or death? If so, how did you go about it? Perhaps sharing some of the decision-making problems would be helpful for the persons in the group.

Have you discussed terminal illness? Have your parents discussed their preferences?

When I think about my parents it should not be merely in terms of what are my responsibilities, but also, do I have enough contact with my parents to enjoy them and appreciate their experience?

Some of us plan vacations that take us to various family groups. We may not get enough time to relax and sit on the front porch with our own dad and mother.

Recently I was privileged to make a speech in my home state at a women's church convention. Part of my planning included a visit for a week with my widowed father. We sat on the front porch and talked and discussed the problems of the church and the exploding crisis of Watergate. I saw him in his relationships with the people of his community. It was a relaxed, satisfying time in which we could catch up with each other.

Many older people have found a new stage in their own lives which we might miss by our narrow perceptions. It is easy to look on both children *and* parents as responsibilities, not persons to enjoy. Such an attitude is hardly loving and also robs us of much of the pleasure life can offer.

A woman of seventy was chatting recently at the health salon which she attends several times a week. "I'm trying to take off ten pounds by exercising so I can go on a cruise and put it all back on." She was delighted with the stage in life she was experiencing. With amusement she told of those who were sponsoring the cruise, a group of retired people. One of their group was recently asked by a member of a singles club, "Do you have anyone who could speak to our group on the subject, 'Is There Anything After Retirement?' " This woman laughed heartily, pointing out that the popular image of old people as senile and ill represents only a small minority—perhaps 5 percent of people over sixty-five.

Marriage Partners and Our Children

In the following chapter we shall consider our most intimate relationships and some of the critical issues related to our life as sexual human beings. Here we want to emphasize that the very immediate relationships with our marriage partner and children—for those of us who are married—are the daily core and substance of our lives. We can't emphasize too much how important they are to us.

Although some people are not currently married, some who live alone do have children, or do care about nieces and nephews. They may have an ex-spouse and children living somewhere else, so that family matters are of deep concern to them. Some people are separated, divorced, or widowed. Some are single adults heading a family of children. Or they may be two women and their children living together sharing expenses and responsibilities. More unusual is the larger group, the extended family which used to be so common.

One middle-aged couple has taken on a variety of responsibilities. Each of them has one parent living. For one parent they built a small apartment joined to their house. The other parent lives in a garage apartment they already had. One of their married children is at home, attending college. The woman takes care of her tiny granddaughter while the daughter goes to college. This couple together have a tremendous responsibility, but have arranged their lives so that each person has some privacy and a room to herself or himself.

Some of the people who are closest to us are our children. Maybe we forget to enjoy them as friends because we know them so well and are so aware of our responsibilities in relation to them.

As teen-agers grow into the early twenties, as they get jobs and go off to school, or set up housekeeping in an apartment or their own home, there are subtle changes.

One woman said of her eighteen-year-old son who suddenly got married, "I'm going through a change in my view of him. About all we had been saying to one another was on the level of 'get your feet off the coffee table.' Now we are talking about their apartment, what they need, about the jobs he and his wife have, about the old kitchen dishes they can use for everyday. It is a real switch—to see him as an adult when he is just fresh out of high school."

As the years pass, we do try to shift gears in our relationships with the young adults. At first they need our support in many ways: the support of letters when they are off at college, the support of consolation and perhaps financial aid if there is a crisis. Then as they become more and more self-sufficient our relationship gets to be more that of an interested friend. We share anecdotes and happenings with them and they with us.

Sometimes one of our children does not keep close contact with us which hurts deeply. But, in wisdom, we try to be there and show interest, and let them know we care—even when they make no moves to meet us. Sometimes a young person needs a breather to find herself or himself. Then after a period of distance, they seem more comfortable with us as parent/friends.

The Family Today

Although there is a great deal of bad publicity and handwringing about the family, I believe there are some healthy trends.

With all the moaning about deterioration of the family, it is hardly noticed that 85 to 90 percent of married people are still continuing in their first marriage and that 70 to 75 percent of people married before are in their second marriage.

Thus, people aim for marriage . . . regard it as a desirable goal and will try again for success if one marriage fails or ends in death of a partner.

Trends in the Family

So many things have changed in the last decade pertaining to the family that it would be helpful to view some of the most important changes that affect us.

The trend toward smaller families. Although we in the middle years had our families before the current trend started, we have internalized some of the thinking that makes the trend reasonable. Recently some of us with large families have been made to feel defensive about the number of children we have.

We know that there is a need to control the world's population in order to feed all the people of the world. We know that with higher prices, recession and depression pressing us, it is difficult to provide our families with the style of living we want for them.

Now that women are finding more years to live and more options for their mature years, it makes sense for them to plan ahead for their non-childcaring years. Men, too, are becoming more involved with a broader range of activities relating to the family and do not look to a large family as a source of pride or machismo. Even though we already have our families, the trend toward zero population growth has encouraged some adult men to get vasectomies. The psychological acceptance of population control has encouraged acceptance of this means of birth control. It benefits not only men, but women who still have the ability to procreate into their forties.

The trend toward equalitarian marriage or partnership marriage. This is a marriage based on three qualities:

a. consensus
b. cooperation
c. communication

The image I like to use is not that of a seesaw—which implies if one is up, the other is down. But the image of a team of horses, pulling together, suggests the closeness of teamwork.

It means that women and men can share in outside work and activities as well as the home responsibilities.

For those who adopt this pattern, it means that more and more sharing in decision-making is the experience and expectation. Adults today realize that many men need the emotional satisfactions of being involved with their children, and many women need the self confidence that comes from being productive in ways other than childbearing and child-rearing.

The two-person commitment, according to the famous sex researchers Masters and Johnson, is the best way to relate to each other. Most people believe that partnership, with a great deal of communication, is the best way to run a marriage.

Sometimes people still quote the old saying, "There can't be two chiefs in a marriage." Today mature adults are likely to reply that there may not be two chiefs but there can be two equal partners, who are considerate and care for each other.

Just as it took two persons to decide to marry—that is, they reached a consensus—intelligent, devoted people find that two persons can reach a consensus on almost anything if they really try.

And, if the issue at question happens to be one they can't resolve, then it is highly doubtful that a decision should be controlled by one person if the other is extremely upset or resentful about it. That is, if one person has a job opportunity that would be advantageous, but the other person is seriously opposed for valid reasons, then it probably would not be a good move. Many couples have found to their dismay that financial success or moving up in the company are not the only values to be weighed.

Cooperation, consensus, and communication are good themes or guidelines for happy relationships.

A shift in marital values. An article in *Psychology Today* tells of changing American attitudes over the past twenty years.

Consider, for example, that in the years since the Civil Rights debates and decision of the fifties and sixties a general acceptance has occurred in our thinking about minorities and education. More than 70 percent of people now believe that education should be integrated, while only 30 percent believe that housing should be integrated. But attitudes do change.

Over a twenty-year period a study in the Detroit area with a cross section of 1,800 adults showed that what people value in marriage has changed.

When people were asked about marriage values, companionship ranked the highest among values desired in marriage. But in 1955 only 48 percent put this first.

In 1971, 60 percent put companionship first. People want the marriage partner to be a "best friend."

The chance to have children dropped in value during this period. In 1955, 70 percent of women wanted three or four children.

In 1971, most women wanted only two children. Today there are some young couples who say they want no children at all. In our growing up period this stance would have been unheard of.

A part of the shift in marital values is what two University of Texas professors have called "intersex convergence." This means that people are recognizing that women and men are more alike than they are different.

Drs. Alice Whatley and Victor Appel say that people are growing more alike in their thinking about sex roles and about family life issues. Whereas we had been taught or conditioned to exaggerate sex characteristics, now people of both sexes are inclined to think more alike than ever before.

Many of us are discovering that all characteristics are human characteristics rather than being clearly defined as feminine or masculine. Both women and men can be strong, weak, mean, aggressive, nurturing, gentle, or clever. Both can be attractive, ugly, competitive, complaining, or weak. What this humanizing trend means is that it is more acceptable for us to be ourselves, to like ourselves. And in marriage, not to insist the other person be the opposite of what we conceive as our own role.

Friends

A more open acceptance of people as people also has a relationship to another group we care about—our friends.

We can accept other people for what they are rather than insist that only certain types of people are "right" for us. We don't have to seek only those people who are homogeneous. We can have some off-beat friends who may stimulate us more than people who are similar to us.

How do you feel about your circle of friends? Do you have several close friends, a wide group of social contacts that know you very well? Are there ways you would like to relate to other people that you have not explored?

Some of us feel so oppressed by the circle of business or professional friends we have that we find no time to make new ones of our own choosing. Some of us have avoided all "groups" and keep only to the one or two persons we have learned to trust over the years.

Does the intersex convergence idea suggest a new dimension to friendship? Are we free to have friends of the opposite sex as well as our own sex? Most single people have a more natural pattern of crossing sex boundaries as far as friends go. Once married, we feel that our contacts with the opposite sex must be limited to people we know at the job, meet at church, or some similar activity. We probably do not feel free to have lunch with a person of the opposite sex other than our marriage partner—unless the person is a well-known friend.

Nena and George O'Neill suggested in their book *Open Marriage* that it is enriching to have friends of the opposite sex. What do you think of their ideas? Even if they make suggestions that are not consistent with one's own moral judgments, their book has solid ideas about refusing to get trapped in an exclusive "Couple Marriage" which means that if one partner can't or won't go somewhere, the other does not go either. Obviously this sort of closed marriage would rob each marriage partner of sports, hobbies, trips, or even business arrangements the other could not share.

What do you think about the issue of sharing all activities? Should you share all friends?

How should social plans be made in a twosome—either dating of singles or in marriage?

Caring in a World Crisis

Although we are acutely conscious of our own economic needs and the critical economic situation in our own country, we are also aware that people in many areas of the world are existing in extreme poverty, hunger, and starvation. So frequently do we see images in magazines, newspapers and on television of emaciated faces and hands reaching out with empty bowls that we almost cringe as we try to imagine what their lives are like. We may feel like turning channels or at least turning away.

We cannot shrug off the situations in these areas of Africa and Asia that are so desperate—yet what can we do?

Are we responsible for helping their countries? We know that we represent 6 percent of the world's population who uses up about two thirds of the world's goods. We cannot square that fact with our despairing feeling that there is not much we can do to help our brothers and sisters across the globe.

Consider what we can do. Are there groups in your own church who are sending money and supplies overseas? There are several church relief agencies that are highly respected for their efficiency and their cost/benefit ratios. That is, less of the money we give goes to pay for fancy offices and high salaries; more goes directly to people in need and communities who need help in agriculture, service agencies, health care agencies, and counseling.

Are there community groups you are familiar with who are working in this area of concern?

Does your congregation or civic group sponsor ideas like Meatless Meals for Hunger Appeal—an attempt to show people what it is like not to have food every meal, and to encourage people to donate the money they would have spent on meat for that meal?

One college president reports that when students were given the choice of a regular cafeteria meal or a "poverty meal" of rice and bread in another dining room, over two hundred chose to experience the poverty meal. The difference in meal cost was to be donated to one church's appeal for funds.

One of the most recent surveys of church leaders in one denomination reports that of all issues and causes concerning these people, World Hunger was at the top of the list. Caring, although it begins with *caring about me,* has to branch out to all God's creatures.

Matthew 25 embodies this concept from Jesus. Inasmuch as we do it unto one of the least of these, we do it unto Jesus.*

---

*See *Christian Century,* March 26, 1975, p. 320, for ordering a 12-page reprint of articles on hunger which will help church groups, ministerial associations, school and college classes better understand today's critical situation.

5.

Who Are You Intimate With?

RACHEL CONRAD WAHLBERG

Middle age—far from being a dreaded milepost in life—is one of the best periods, insist writers Morton and Bernice Hunt, who became husband and wife when they were in their early fifties.

"We think the first step on the road to enjoyment of middle age is simply to have the concept that it's the prime time of your life," says Bernice Kohn Hunt, who has written many non-fiction books for young people.

Morton Hunt, who wrote *Sexual Behavior in the 1970s,* adds, "The new middle age is a post-parental, high-achievement time, with good health and more leisure, when people can fulfill themselves doing things they care about. It's a time of renewed and heightened intimacy for a couple."

Mrs. Hunt points out that the average woman has had the last child she will have by age thirty and is therefore relatively young when the last child leaves home.

"Mommy and daddy can stop being mommy and daddy and get back to each other."

Morton Hunt believes that one reason middle age is less terrifying today is that old age has become less terrifying. "With Social Security, Medicaid, and Medicare you can live

93

and enjoy yourself and not always be worrying about the future."

The fifty-five-year-old Hunt points out that the mental processes do not decline, as is popularly believed. He learned how to play tennis in his mid-forties and had never played the piano until three years ago when Bernice began to teach him.

These two mature bright spirits believe that the women's movement has changed the balance of male-female relationships. Says Morton, "A man welcomes a woman sharing in the achieving of income and who maintains an interest in things outside the home. This pays off later when instead of having a wife who changes the decor every two years and haunts the doctor's office, the man has a companion. Men are learning that this is a time marriage can be better sexually and psychologically than ever."

Sex, too, becomes a disquieting factor in middle years. Generally, after fifty, the average male believes his virility is waning. Depressed, he is unlikely to take it gracefully and may fall back on physical fatigue as an alibi. Dreading a loss of manliness—and to boost his ego—a middle-ager may be prone to seek extramarital affairs. But medical authorities point out that the prime sex problem is emotional, not physical; that middle age means a slowing down of sexual activity in men, not an ending of functions.

Women in this age bracket may suffer a feeling of loss at the "empty nest," when grown children leave home, but many are really relieved because they have discharged their responsibilities and can now turn to new activities. With more freedom, they tend to become expansive and socially engaged.

The woman in middle years will ask herself, "Am I still attractive?" as wrinkles appear, hair gets thin, and waistline tends to bulge. She, too, is ruffled by teens. "I can't even talk to Johnny any more," or "Susy is always telling me how to dress," are common complaints. The middle-aged woman worries less about her own health than her husband's and starts to pay more attention to him in his care and feeding.

Despite being proud of her home and family, there may come a time when a woman wonders, "What have I *done* with my life?"

Theodore Irwin in *Family Weekly* offers these suggestions for enjoying your middle years:

• Size yourself up frankly. Accept your limitations. Remember your self-image changes during the forties and fifties. To find contentment, even if you feel you have not achieved all you set out to do, the sensible approach is to match your aspirations to reality.

• Strike out on a newly productive path, Harvard's eminent psychiatrist, Dr. Erik Erikson, counsels. It's a time for rebirth. Find new diversions, exciting and absorbing interests, whether it's civic activities or new hobbies. Take advantage of your increasing leisure to broaden yourself intellectually.

• Concede that physical changes do occur, but don't assume that disabilities are inevitable. Many people reach a late age without incurring a heart attack or other major illnesses. Watch your diet, take prudent exercise.

• For men, take a fresh look at your job or profession to uncover new insights and satisfactions.

• In the last analysis, whatever the focus of annoyance or stress, aware middle-agers should bear in mind that they are still the powerful Command Generation—in their second and important "prime of life."

What Do We Mean By Our Sexuality?

We have come a long way in our openness in discussing subjects that were once taboo. Here are some headlines from clippings gleaned in the last few months:

> THREE GREAT MYTHS OF SEX AND SPORT
> RELIGION VS. SEXUALITY
> BACK TO A NEW "MIDDLE" IN SEX
> PROSTITUTION RULING LANDS MEN IN JAIL
> BIRTH CONTROL DISCUSSED
> RAPE PROSECUTION CHANGES PROPOSED

WHAT WE KNOW ABOUT THE PILL

INSIDE AN ABORTION CLINIC

ARTIFICIAL INSEMINATON EXPLAINED

ABORTION AND THE TRUE BELIEVER

RX: SEX FOR ZEST OVER SIXTY

Most of these subjects would not have been common discussion topics in our parents' day. One of the trends of the last two decades has been an openness about ourselves as sexual human beings.

All of us need to love and be loved. No matter what our age, we need love and affection, the sense that we belong in relation to other people.

One outstanding psychologist points out that there are varying needs—or a hierarchy of needs. That is, if our basic need for food and drink is denied, we will pay attention to that need rather than our need to write a poem.

Thus:

- physical needs come first;
- then social needs, belonging to a group, being accepted . . . security;
- then needs for achievement or self fulfillment;
- then higher ambitions, for knowledge, for creative achievement.

We have recognized that we care for other people. We love people, have affection for them, wish them well. But it is not just a one-way sort of feeling. In normal human beings, this sense of caring must flow mutually back and forth; it must be returned.

The baby responds to the parents who love her or him. We continue to love our own parents, brothers, and sisters, the people in our immediate relationships.

Even at a distance, we continue to care for people.

There are many ways we satisfy our need for intimacy with others. And there are many degrees of intimacy. Whether we are married or not, we need intimate relationships with others.

The persons who are single, divorced, separated, widowed—all need intimate friends and relationships.

Just how we become intimate with another is rather mysterious. As Martin Buber has pointed out, when we enter a relationship with another person, we wait for an invitation from that other person who stands at a distance from us.

When we are young we sometimes make the mistake of thinking that love means only intimacy—and we interpret that as being so close to each other that there is hardly breath in between.

But "relation presupposes both distance (or distinctness) and presentness," points out Reuel Howe. If we try to lose ourselves in the other, such immersion in another destroys the possibility of relationship, the polarity necessary for dialogue, the polarity we mean by distance.

Both presentness and distance are especially required, says Howe. If there is to be a dialogue, each person must be apart and distinct. Otherwise, abnormal dependence of one upon the other or any blurring of the distinctness impairs the relationship.

What we are saying is that two-individual-but-whole-persons achieve intimacy. If one is totally dependent on the other, there is no spark, no interchange. Who wants a shadow of himself or herself as a friend or companion?

All of us have experienced a growth of insight, or a burst of understanding after a conversation with other persons that could not have been produced by one person alone. As two or more persons share and care, they become more than they were before.

A Negative Historical Perspective

For many centuries Christians taught and believed that sexuality—or the need for intimacy—was a part of life that should be suppressed.

There were ancient ideas that contributed to this position. Christianity came into being during a period when people thought human beings had two sides or parts to their personalities. There was the higher existence which was understood to be the mental, spiritual life, and there was the lower existence which was identified with sexual yearnings.

Because males were the ones who wrote, studied, preached, and transmitted the thought of those centuries, it was the experience of men that was transmitted. Some of these ancient respected philosophers and fathers of the church associated sex with sin. And obviously, if one counted sex as sin, the one who was doing the reasoning associated the sexual partner—woman—with the sexual part of life that must be put down.

Augustine is a good example of this "sex-as-sin mystique." Not only was he influenced by Manichaeism, a philosophy which emphasized the dualism of flesh and spirit, but he felt guilty about his own sexual experience. From the age of nineteen to twenty-eight Augustine had lived with a woman out of wedlock and afterwards had intense feelings of guilt about the relationship. His own sense of guilt hardened his views against sex and against woman as sexual partner. If one must put down sex, then one must put down women. Augustine identified sexual intercourse in marriage as "the greatest threat to spiritual freedom." "Only the possibility of pregnancy," he concluded, "justifies the conjugal act. I do not see what other help women would be to man, if the purpose of generating would be eliminated."

This sort of thinking, built on the Eve Mystique, was supported by passages from Paul and other biblical writers. That is, all women are Eves and that Eve was more to blame for sin than Adam. Although the creation story in Genesis 1 declares both male and female were made in God's image, that fact is frequently lost in overemphasis on the rib story in Genesis 2 and 3, and in overemphasis on punishment and subordination.

Christians have had a hard time dealing with their sexuality in positive ways because there is so much negative support in Scripture for a negative view. How do we deal with selections like these:

- It is better not to touch a woman (1 Cor. 7:1).
- It is better to marry than to burn (1 Cor. 7:9).
- Woman must cover her head; man ought not for he is the image of God, but the woman is the glory of man (1 Cor. 11:3).
- Let women keep quiet in the church . . . it is shameful for women to speak in church (1 Cor. 14:34,35).
- Women are not to teach or have authority over men. For Adam was formed first, then Eve, and Adam was not deceived but the woman was . . . Yet woman will be saved through childbirth if she continues in faith and charity and holiness with modesty (2 Tim. 2:8-15).

During the Reformation period, even Calvin and Luther had trouble justifying some of these passages. Regarding Adam being first, Calvin said, "It is obvious that firstness does not mean superiority. John the Baptist preceded Jesus and that didn't make him superior." Indeed, women might point out that being created last might mean being created as *the climax of creation*—not an afterthought. And the writer of Timothy in saying Eve was chiefly to blame, not Adam, runs contrary to Genesis which describes mutual guilt, and contrary to Romans 5 in which Paul declared that as sin came into the world through one man—Adam—so by one man's obedience—Christ—many will be made righteous.

Although Martin Luther did marry and believed that priests should marry, he had many antiquated attitudes regarding women. "Eve's sorrow," he said, "which she would not have had if she had not fallen into sin, are to be great, numerous, and of various kinds. The female sex bears a far severer and harsher punishment than the men." After describing vividly the discomforts of pregnancy and the sixteenth century horrors of childbirth, Luther asks, "For what is there of such things a man suffers?"

Like Augustine, Luther also saw sexual activity in marriage as tainted with shame and guilt. He writes, "It is a great favor that God has preserved woman for us against our wish and will, as it were—both for procreation and also as a medicine against the sin of fornication. In paradise woman would have been a help only . . . but now she is an antidote and a medicine." Like Paul, Luther regarded marriage as a protection against sin, a secondary option; if you can't control yourself, then marry.

Said Luther, "We can hardly speak of woman without a feeling of shame, and surely we cannot make use of her without shame." His phrase "make use of her" reminds us of the Playboy philosophy that regards woman as a sex object.

Today we are seeing that this whole approach to our human sexuality, with its negative ideas about women, was wrong-headed and destructive. Rosemary Reuther, in her writings, ("Sexism and the Theology of Liberation," *Christian Century*, December 12, 1973, and *Liberation Theology*, Paulist Press, 1972), describes *sexism as sin:*

> Social alienation begins in self-alienation, experienced as an estrangement between the self and the body. The oppressive relationship of the man to the woman is essentially a social projection of the self-alienation that translates certain initial biological differences into a power relationship. This relationship in turn is [reflected] in social structures and cultural modes that eliminate woman's autonomous personhood to define her solely in terms of male needs and negations.
>
> In classical times, [it] took the form of an identification of women with the "lower half" of self-alienated experience. Woman was stultifying matter over against male intellectuality. Woman was emotionality, sexuality, over against male spirituality.

She goes on to say that these images became self-fulfilling as women internalized the images they received socially, and these ideas were reinforced by exclusion of women from education and participation in public life.

To forbid woman enlarging cultural experiences is to internalize these self-images in her, to make her *be* what she symbolizes to self-alienated male perception.

Thus what has happened is that a fear of sexuality has developed. Not only do we experience this as an alienation of mind from body, but male-female relations are "envisioned as a kind of social extension of mind-body relations. This implies a subject-object or I-It relation between men and women sexually.

If women are identified as a "sex object," either rightly used for procreation or wrongly abused for carnal pleasure, then in neither case does woman appear as a person.

The Struggle to Affirm Sexuality

Even though we know now that the old approaches were wrong—on physical, psychological and theological/spiritual grounds—it is very difficult for modern society and religion to tear itself away from some of the oppressive and destructive patterns.

- Women and girls are still encouraged to dress and decorate themselves as sex objects.
- Advertisers still use women as bait or decorations to sell their products. Recent studies done by business marketing professors at the University of Delaware and at Queens College in New York, indicate a lessening use of women as sex objects in television commercials and magazine advertising. Although women are usually portrayed at home or in subservient roles, there is a slight increase in the number of men shown in the home.
- Men are encouraged to find their identification with "Marlboro Men" and football heroes, rather than as

nurturing human beings with warm relationships with women and children.

- In Christian practices, women are still excluded from most "up front" activity, although more and more churches are ordaining women, offering courses in sex education, male/female roles, changing life-styles, and moral-ethical questions.

In contrast to negative Scripture passages, many writers are discovering positive passages in which human sexuality is affirmed. Again and again Jesus treated all people as the real human beings they were without labeling them as the first-century society did. (See Krister Stendhal's *Bible and the Role of Women,* Fortress Press; Georgia Harkness, *Women in Church and Society,* Abingdon; Rachel Conrad Wahlberg, *Jesus According to a Woman,* Paulist Press; Letty M. Russell's *Human Liberation in a Feminist Perspective—a Theology,* Westminster, and others). One of the best small paperbacks, although written to meet the crisis in the Episcopal church concerning women's ordination, has the most complete clustering together of formal and informal arguments about the woman/man issue in church and society. It is *Women Priests: Yes or No?* by Emily C. Hewitt and Suzanne R. Hiatt.

Although we live in a sexually charged age, we do not thereby have genuine sexual freedom or a great deal of sexual pleasure. Rather, the sexual revolution we have heard so much about seems to be more one of looser language than of freer life-style—or acceptance of our own sexual needs and pleasures.

Under our barrage of sexy words, movies, magazines, and a variety of stimulating images, most of us are still fairly frightened of sexuality—and especially of genuine intimacy with someone else. To deny the need for intimacy is to deny the power of the life God gave us; it is to turn against the depths of being. We know now that our sexuality is not in any sense evil, but that sexuality, like everything else in life, can be abused and used to create evil situations.

The Swing Back from Sexual Freedom

What did we mean by sexual freedom anyway? The advent of fairly reliable birth control measures was accompanied with a great feeling of relief. There was a booming period of freedom when men and women seemed to feel: Now we don't have to worry about reproduction; we can enjoy sex.

When the Pill first came on the market in 1960, the awareness that this simple form of birth control was now available on a mass basis was mind-blowing. Following awareness came a period of intense interest. A large percentage of women asked their doctors to prescribe the Pill and for several years it was regarded as the greatest boon to sexual relations since the beginning of history.

During this period, many other forms of contraception were almost abandoned—the diaphragm, the intrauterine devices, the condom, etc. Then in a wave of medical doubts and scare articles about bloodclotting and ailments seemingly related to the use of the Pill, many women backed off, were advised to use another birth control method until more research was done.

Today the pendulum has swung back to a middle position, with general acceptance of the Pill, especially its improved forms, and with attention given to other methods of birth control.

The fact remains that American couples feel freed from the tyranny of their reproductive organs. For the first time in history, people can choose whether to have children or not. And men, for their part, have increasingly accepted the availability of vasectomies. From an attitude of hush-hush a few years ago, men are now openly talking about their vasectomies. Rather than subject the woman to thirty years of contraceptives, many couples feel that it is reasonable for the man to have a thirty-minute operation once the family has the desired number of children.

A good book to read on the subject of male and female sterilization is *Foolproof Birth Control* by Lawrence Lader,

Beacon Press. Lader cites studies which show that despite scare articles about psychological upsets to men who have vasectomies, unless a man was already psychologically disturbed, there are almost no dangers to men who choose vasectomy.

Lader also has excellent chapters, supported by many medical charts and data, on "Female Sterilization: How It Affects a Woman's Physical and Mental Health, Sexual Life, and Marriage," and "Tubal Ligation." Results of medical and psychological surveys show that no immediate postoperative physical complications were found in 92 percent of the women studied. Psychological findings reported indicate that sexual relations are substantially not affected by sterilization, while the sterilized patients experience a marked improvement in their expressed level of happiness.

What seems to be happening is a swing toward responsibility, and away from an overabundance of sexual freedom. After the first bursts of liberation from the constraints imposed on women and men because of their procreative ability, a sense of responsibility and good sense seems to be prevailing.

Perhaps the problem was that for a decade or so people were confusing *freedom* with *license*. True freedom must be tempered with judgment and responsibility. In contrast, *license* —kicking over the traces entirely—implies no fences, no constraints, no wisdom.

Dr. Amitai Etzioni, a Columbia University sociologist, said in a speech to the American Association for the Advancement of Science (AAAS): "The celebrated sexual direction of the sixties is losing its appeal and some of the swingers who followed it have discovered that the journey wasn't so thrilling after all." This is what Dr. Etzioni discovered after interviews with 215 Greenwich Village singles and 50 couples at Rutgers University who lived together and then decided to marry.

"Increasingly the separation of sex from affection is being discovered by the avant-garde of sexual liberation to result in frustration, tension, and jealousy." Etzioni predicts that the movement of American society toward reducing sex to animal-like conduct between people is about to end. He feels that "the pendulum, after swinging perilously close to sexual anarchy in the 1960s is swinging back to a new synthesis, a new middle."

New Definitions of Sexuality

What people seem to be discovering is that sex without caring, sharing, love and commitment—is a rather meaning-less game. People are rejecting the body-for-pleasure type of thinking exemplified by *Playboy* and *Playgirl* magazines. To titillate the lusty sense with centerfold pictures of nude bodies—male or female—is one thing. But to enter an inter-personal relationship with no more depth of feeling than is encouraged by such publications, leaves one empty.

Because William Masters and Virginia Johnson are highly respected scientists in the field of sexuality, their book, *The Pleasure Bond,* with its emphasis on commitment, made quite an impact.

What does it mean to be committed? these doctors ask. "Put in its simplest terms, a commitment is a pledge to do something."

"Caring flows from two related but different kinds of feelings. One is a feeling of being *responsive to* someone, of *caring for* someone, of wanting to take care of him or her. These feelings are generated in entirely different ways. Re-sponsiveness occurs spontaneously, before the mind is con-sciously aware of what is happening—a sudden surge of interest and attraction triggered by another person's physical presence. Responsibility is consciously, though often unwill-ingly, invoked by the mind—an acknowledgment of obliga-tion."

According to Masters and Johnson, the pleasure bond begins in infancy when a child is dependent on parents, but both receive mutual benefit and pleasure from each other.

"It is this search for pleasure—and pleasure is an infinitely deeper and more complex emotional matter than simple sensual gratification—that continues throughout life.

"When there is more displeasure than pleasure in a marriage, a husband and wife are more aware of the obligations of marriage than they are of its rewards, and their bond can be characterized as a commitment of obligation.

"In contrast there is the commitment of concern, a bond in which a man and a woman mutually meet their obligations not because they feel compelled to do so but because they feel impelled to, by impulse, desires and convictions that are deeply rooted in themselves."

The new definition of sexuality, then, must include commitment and caring on a broader, deeper level than mere enjoyment of sex. To make a commitment to someone is to become a steadfast friend and ally. It is at once an act of faith and an acceptance of vulnerability.

Think for a moment about the person you are most intimate with. Can you explain the way you began to turn toward each other? In a marvelous way you began drawing together in communion with one another. For the Christian, sexuality is a gift from God, an experience of spirituality as well as physical closeness.

As two people, you began to delight in each other, in the presence and conversation of each other, in touching and affection, in sharing ideals and interpretations of daily events.

You found that sharing discussion—even differences—was stimulating and enriching. And so you grew together, yet remained two private individuals with some distance between.

Divorce—and Singleness

Of course many people do not have mutual relationships that grow into satisfying marriages. Part of the attempt at sexual freedom for some persons was a frustrated experiencing of one marriage after another—of "serial monogamy." Or a series of heterosexual sharings that did not last.

Some people have resigned themselves to a lack of intimacy in an economic arrangement which they call "marriage"— either for the sake of the children, or for the sake of social approval. A recent book by a Rockefeller daughter-in-law explains how desperately she sought to hold the marriage together because of her own insecurity and because her husband was such a good father to the children.

Mel Krantzler, author of the popular *Creative Divorce* says 25 percent of all divorces involve people wed fifteen years or more. In the last five years the number of divorces among couples married twenty years or longer has increased 50 percent, according to George Williams, executive director of Parents Without Partners, the largest organization for single parents.

Although most divorced persons feel there is a fantasy image about divorce that encourages people to think they are "swingers" having a good time, the reverse is true. There are many problems and frustrations in working out relationships from the previous years, in caring for children, in finding new groups and new friends, in fighting loneliness.

Despite the desire that most people have for a stable marriage situation, many people choose to live alone. The number of people living alone now totals 13.3 million out of a population of about 213 million. The number of people living alone has jumped three million over the last five years, with 23 percent of the increase coming in the most recent year.

With 69,000,000 households in the nation, that means 19.1 percent of the households consist of one person living alone. Five years ago, when households numbered 61,000,000 that percentage was 16.7.

People sixty-five and over still represent the largest chunk of the live-alone population: 5.7 million. But 46 percent of the increase over the last five years has been in the youngest of the three census brackets. The number of people under thirty-five living alone is now 2.7 million. Thus there are:

- people who are divorced or separated;
- young people who choose to live by themselves;
- older people living alone;
- people in any age level who have never married.

What we are seeing is a lessening of pressures on people to do the conventional thing—get married. There are other options, other choices. People can choose to live alone. And they can choose to be very cautious about another marriage if they are divorced.

Shifting Sex Role Patterns

Because of the lessening cultural emphasis on housewifery, maternity, and marriage, life patterns for both women and men are changing.

Dr. Suzanne Keller, professor of sociology at Princeton University, writes in a magazine for psychiatrists, *Reflection,* that she sees several trends which contribute to the changing sex roles of women:

- the shape of the economy which favors a stationary population;
- acceptance of the Pill and fertility control among all religious groups;
- changing attitudes and policies toward abortion;
- genetic intervention in conception and gestation;
- the drop in the birth rate to its lowest point in American history, to below replacement level;
- breakthroughs for women in unusual spheres of work;
- the feminist movement.

Dr. Keller notes that commitment to interesting work does seem to compete successfully with having children and is thus conducive to the nationally desirable lowered fertility.

Because of our tendency to see self-reliance and hard thinking as masculine attributes, it will take some social conditioning to show most people that ambition, independence and success are not gender-based characteristics at all.

"To date, these traits have been monopolized by the male

role, but certainly not by all men—thereby helping to structure personality by gender. But, in the future, as sex roles are revised under the pressure of new priorities, this artificial restriction of capacities should cease. The earlier we start to develop new self-images among women, the more firmly these will become anchored in the psyche and the more swiftly the transition to new patterns of life will occur."

A recent Supreme Court ruling indicates that men are benefiting as well as women by some legal changes. The government, says this ruling, must pay Social Security benefits to widowers as well as widows when they are left with children in their care.

In an 8 to 0 decision, the court said a federal law restricting the benefits to widows is unconstitutional sex discrimination.

Justice William Brennan said, "It is no less important for a child to be cared for by its sole surviving parent when the parent is male rather than female."

"Their sexual contouring as children" points out Germaine Greer in a recent interview, "moves them away from a life of tenderness and dependency into 'manly' conquistadorial roles. It's really very difficult for men—especially for the nice ones."

In an article provocatively called "Why Women Lose," Dr. Thomas Boslooper and Marcia Hayes point out that women don't know how to win or how to compete, "and they're programmed not to try."

These attitudes in women toward competition and success are established early, say the authors. "Infant girls are handled differently from boys—more affectionately, more protectively. And as soon as they learn to walk, girls are trained differently. Sociologists John Roberts and Brian Sutton Smith confirmed this in a cross-cultural study of 1,900 elementary school children given a variety of psychological tests and interviews.

Perhaps the ideal arrangement, as we broaden our sex role concepts, is an arrangement of two persons based on co-responsibility as a theme. Co-marriage might well be the

concept that replaces the power arrangement of patriarchy—
or male supremacy.

There will be more of a spirit of co-responsibility across the
board: *Support* will be broadened to mean "co-responsibility":

- in earning money
- in job status
- in care of home
- in care of children
- in development of abilities
- in sexual pleasure
- in socializing—self, couple, and children.

Rather than thinking of each other as equally powerful,
we may be open to the idea that we are primarily equally
vulnerable. Vulnerable to love and need, vulnerable to caring,
vulnerable to mistakes, vulnerable to growth.

This could be the ideal fulfillment, the ideal intimacy.

6.

What Can I Do?

JOHN C. COOPER

One might very well ask why we should pay consideration to our entry into middle life? Perhaps the best thing to do is to ignore it. Apparently, a large number of people in our society feel this way. Some psychologists say that the chief problem involved in becoming middle-aged is simply becoming middle-aged. A major issue in the study of middle life, as we saw in the first chapter, is to establish just what middle life means.

But let us assume that we have established just what middle life means. Let us assume that there is some worth to be derived from investigating our situation in the world with its responsibilities, opportunities, and challenges. What then? By this time are we so set in our ways, so compromised by "The System," or so totally bound by obligations and mortgages that there is little we can do but sigh in our chains.

In order to make a study of middle life meaningful, we must assume that there are some options left open to us, some possibilities of freedom, some choices of the better over the worse.

How can we validate this feeling that we have options? Certainly a great many of us feel that our options are considerably limited by now. How much freedom is actually left?

Every generation could ask and has asked these questions. But particularly in this latter portion of the twentieth century, millions of people, from various sub-groups of the general population, are asking about the dimensions of control left to them over their own lives. In this chapter we want to investigate our attitudes toward freedom and help you to understand the possibilities of change—for the better—that still exist for those of us in middle life. The great philosopher Immanuel Kant once said that one could not logically prove that human beings were free, nevertheless, each of us inwardly feel that we are free and that our choices make a real difference in the world. If we do feel free, then we are free.

Have you ever asked yourself, "What dimensions of control do I have over my own life?" How much freedom do any of us really have? How much freedom do you want to have that you have given up? If you feel you once had freedom or more freedom than now and gave it up, do you feel resentful?

What Do I Really Want from Life?

We must consider the possibility of change, even when we are convinced that there is no way for us to really control anything other than perhaps what we will have for supper or the clothes we wear. I believe we still have a feeling that we could change things somewhat if we wished. But the way North American society is set up, we think of the possibility of change almost in financial terms.

We realize that if we were to win the Michigan Sweepstakes, the Ohio Lottery, or the Ontario Grand Prize, we would have the money to do what we wanted to. When people feel this way, and I suppose that is why so many lottery tickets are sold—even though they may not have a very good idea of what they would like to do—they have the *possibility* of doing what they would like to do.

Finances are a very important part of life. The economic

area is hardly one that the Christian can turn away from. After all, everything that is done in society, not only in North America and Europe but behind the Iron Curtain and in communist countries as well, is done with the aid of money. It is the way in which we judge the power that lies behind ideas, techniques, and inventions. So getting yourself straight about finances and economics isn't a bad thing as you look at yourself in the midst of life.

The fact is, those of us in middle age are at the prime of our earning power. We are essentially the people who own common stock, insurance policies, and have equities built up in our houses. Although our debts may be astronomical, we do have the edge on the younger generation that is just starting out, and in many instances, we have the edge on the older generation who may now be supporting themselves by living off their capital. We should not consider the possibility of change or of doing what we want only in economic terms, but it would be foolish if we did not take economics into account as we consider just what areas of life we can and cannot control.

For a person who feels trapped in a particular situation in life nothing will give him or her more of a sense of independence than having a job. Many housewives today know this feeling because the economic situation of the seventies has forced them to take a job in order to supplement their husbands' income. Sociologists tell us that this is often more of a *feeling* of freedom than actual freedom itself, because so many of the jobs that unskilled women receive do not pay for themselves. There are the added expenses of prepared meals, eating out, babysitters, clothes, transportation, payments to Social Security, income tax, etc. that come along when you do get a second job in the family. Often there is nothing, or little, left of the profits. Knowing this, however, many women still go to work because of the feeling of independence and the sense of self-worth it gives them. We are not suggesting that women should go to work. We are suggesting, however, that it is one option today if you feel trapped, or feel that there is no possibility of change and that you are not able to be in charge of your own destiny.

We must come back again though to the questions, Do we fear change? Do we welcome it? Or do we simply tolerate change? Is there anything at all about myself that I want to change? I suppose just in asking that question we see the foolishness of it, for even the most conservative of us have something we would like to change. We think about a new hairstyle, having it cut, letting it grow, or perhaps we think about new clothes. The new bright colors in men's clothing seem to say to us that we should get a suit like that, too. But in the context of welcoming, fearing, tolerating, or just going along with change, there is also a very important question that Christians must ask. That question is: What would I like to preserve about myself? What is there about me that is going on, in Wesley's terms, "to perfection"? What is there about me that is going on, becoming better, not because of any goodness in me but because of the work of God in my life? What are the evidences of the Holy Spirit's work? What is he changing? What do I fear? And why?

We must come to these questions because anytime one faces a dreadful conundrum—the paradox of freedom and destiny—which some people have called a contradiction of predestination and individual free will, we come down to fear. People very often give themselves over to the stars, believing that all is fixed, that nothing can be changed. Because they fear change, they fear that in lifting up their hands in their own behalf, in the behalf of the rest of mankind, they may do something wrong. And sometimes people claim a total freedom, not taking into account the great parts of life that are directed by God, that are a part of nature, that lie essentially beyond human control, because they do not have any perfect faith and love in God.

We want to ask, too, the question about our vocation. Are we really happy in our jobs? This is not meant to make you unhappy when you are, nor is it meant to cast any aspersions upon the vocations you have elected in life. Our questions are meant only to ask, Is your vocation fulfilling you, making you better, bringing you to a happy and complete fulfillment in life? Is your vocation serving you, your family, your fellowman, and your Lord?

Before Asking, What Can I Do . . .

Before asking, What can I do? each of us must ask ourselves what we really want from life. It's strange, but very few of us have ever really asked ourselves that question. At least we haven't asked the question seriously. When asked, What do you really want from life? we often make light of it. We say "Oh, I'd like to be the Emperor of China," or "I'd like to go to Alaska," or "on a safari in Africa." Perhaps we *would* like to do those things and there wouldn't be anything wrong with it, but are those really the things that lie at the core of our being? What are the elements that make up our personal stories? What have we seen ourselves as being—ever since we were little children and played at being doctor, nurse, and sky pilot. When we played at being grown up perhaps we really said what we wanted to be.

Let's take a moment to perform an experiment. Take a sheet of paper and a pencil, sit down at your kitchen table or desk, or in the front room in the easy chair, and play a little game. Assume that this is your last year to live. Now, with that assumption firmly in mind, list five things you would like to have accomplished before your death. These can be things that you have already done, or projects you are now doing, or completely new things.

Ask yourself, What really is important to me? After having prepared this list you may want to share it with someone else.

Managing Our Time

One of our writers has developed the idea that each of us is living out an inner fantasy. By this, he means that each of us has a kind of scenario that we have set up for ourselves in life, although it could well be that this scenario is subconscious and not recognized at all. This writer is urging us to become aware of the story we are telling ourselves so that we might better understand what has happened to us in the past and will be happening to us in the future. But before we can get control of our inner story, we must get control of our time. Controlling our time represents a challenge that few of us are able to meet.

How many times do we complain that we have no time to ourselves? How often do we have to miss meetings, family opportunities, movies and plays that we would like to be a part of because we simply do not have time? Considering the schedule of families today, it is safe to say that most of us fall into such patterns. Indeed, it appears that the more labor-saving devices and quick-preparation foods that come to us, the busier we are. Not all of us belong to a jet set, but many of the men in our generation do, simply because their work demands such activities. Twenty-seven hour days, flying from the East to the West Coast on business, are familiar experiences for many men in their forties. For all of us, housewives included, hours spent driving along crowded freeways are everyday challenges. The routine of our work and social lives, including all the travel involved, ultimately bore and psychically fatigue us.

For the woman at home, the constant rush of keeping house for a busy family may make her oblivious to her own psychological and physical needs. Like her husband, she is also driven by many anxieties, many of them based on competition in the social world—similar to the business competition her husband faces—that drives her on and on without satisfaction or relief.

Think closely, do you see yourself in this description? Is the flight from anxiety into activity characteristic of your family? We know that many men have this syndrome, do the women have it, also? We see many teen-aged children marked by such anxieties. It is not uncommon to see such anxieties about status and achievement in preteen-age children. All of the sports groups, youth groups, and even some church groups, push us into this drive to excel.

What do you think that the stress on the Cub Scout to earn a recruiter's patch does to the child's enjoyment of scouting? What does the pressure of pastors and Sunday school teachers on youngsters to compete to see who can bring in the most people do to the child's appreciation of Christianity? How healthy and Christian is it to give hamburgers, candy, yo-yos, and balloons to children for coming to Sunday school? Can you imagine how the child who is unable to bring someone must feel? Can you imagine how children in one congregation feel who see their friends lured away by such tactics to another congregation? What kind of concepts of time and control over one's life are given the child—and the parent—by such tactics?

Are you in control of your own time? Sit down with several pieces of paper and make a graph of the twenty-four hours in a day, one for each of the seven days of a typical week. Now fill it in, using ink for the standard activities you must do, and a pencil for activities that vary, are voluntary, or represent free choices. See how much free time you really have.

The desire to climb the social ladder often causes some wives to over-involve themselves in civic, school, and church activities. Adding these activities to the many business, civic, and social activities of the husband, along with the school and social activities of the children, produces a life-style that has no time for family growth and spiritual development. Often there is not even time for the necessary rest the body needs to function well. Sicknesses, family disputes, and other dysfunctions grow out of this madhouse atmosphere. You will never know what you can do or what freedom is open to you, until you master your time. The average middle-class household in our generation resembles a business corporation much more than it does the families of our childhood. We have designed for ourselves an efficient machine to produce divorces, mental breakdowns, and general unhappiness. Unfortunately, too many of our churches are as guilty of fostering this life-style as are the more recognizably selfish groups such as country clubs and business associations.

The importance of having enough time for ourselves is underscored today, not only by the many calls for new life-styles from young people and members of the counter-culture, but also by psychologists. They note that the "fairy tale" that seems to be the life scenario in many American families is ruining mental health and pushing up the suicide rate. Consider the following news story:

"FAIRY TALE" CONCEPT BLAMED FOR TEENAGER SUICIDE HIKE

MILWAUKEE, WIS. Amy, 15, had always gotten straight A's in school, and her parents were extremely upset when she got a B on her report card.

"If I fail in what I do," Amy told her parents, "I fail in what I am."

The message was part of Amy's suicide note.

Dr. Darold Treffert, director of the Winnebago Mental Health Institute at Oshkosh, Wisconsin, places part of the blame for a sharp increase in teen-age suicides on what he calls "The American Fairy Tale."

He says the number of teen-age suicides in the United States has tripled in the last decade, to an estimated thirty a day, and that more than half the patients in the nation's psychiatric hospitals are under age twenty-one.

He says the "fairy tale" has five themes: that more possessions mean more happiness, that a person who does or produces more is more important, that everyone must belong and identify with some larger group, that perfect mental health means no problems and that a person is abnormal unless constantly happy.

"For some, the American Fairy Tale ends in suicide or psychiatric hospitals, but for countless others, it never ends at all," Treffert said during an interview.

He said millions of Americans are plagued throughout their lives by a gnawing emptiness or meaninglessness expressed not as a fear of what may happen to them, but rather as a fear that nothing will happen to them.

He said Americans must stop evaluating themselves according to what they own or what they have done and learn to accept and cope with various mental and emotional problems.

"A whole generation has come to feel that it is unAmerican to experience any of these emotions," he said.

He says parents should avoid trying to make their children live up to the standards of the "fairy tale," and treat them as individuals, as people rather than possessions.

If we are to overcome the kind of evil that we build into our character and life-styles that this news story demonstrates, we must learn to master our time. We must learn that there is time enough for us to do all that is necessary for us to do, there is time enough for us to do all that we truly want to do.

At this point we need to be introduced, not just to a new system of psychology, but to the very idea that there are ways that we can keep everything from being reduced to materialistic terms. Perhaps we should read books like J. Menninger's *Success through Transactional Analysis* (Signet), or Dr. Eric Berne's *Games People Play*, or the book by T.A. Harris, *I'm OK—You're OK*. We need to be reminded that we may be acting out the role of a child or parent who isn't really ourselves as adults, instead of acting out the role of adult who is ourself—that is our ego—in our decision-making as well as our relations with others. We may be living in ways that neither make us happy nor other people happy. We may be making decisions that quietly ask others to "kick me" or that say, "I'm not OK," when we could be saying, "I am OK" and being objective and free. Perhaps you ought to check out the transactional analysis or the psychological system on which "I'm OK—You're OK" is based.

I want to tell you just a bit about the vocabulary of TA here, so that you might possibly use this in thinking about yourself and what you can and can't change about your life. Also, this might be helpful in your thinking about how you can become a master of your time, and come to believe in the realistic view of freedom that is open to us as adults in America.

The essential vocabulary of Transactional Analysis, a new rather popularized view of psychology for the layman, consists of only six terms. They are: transaction, parent, adult, child, OK, and games. Here is a very brief rundown on what these terms mean.

A *transaction* is an exchange between two or more persons. Dr. Eric Berne has said that this is the basic social unit for the study of human behavior, thus, Transactional Analysis is the systematic study of the interactions between human beings.

Parent, adult and *child* are ego-states, and each of us has these three segments of our personalities. The "parent" ego-state is a permanent recording in our brains of the do's and dont's we learned as small children. On the other hand, the "child" is a recording of the feelings we absorbed in our early years. The "adult" is a data computer which surveys and weighs the facts before we make a decision. The "adult" refers directly to our ego, our identity, our personhood, as John, Alice, Edith, or Fred.

An *OK* position is a healthy attitude or voice that enables us to feel positive about ourselves and others. Because of the disappointments and inadequacies we feel as small children growing up in an adult world, most of us reach adulthood with strong "not-OK" feelings. *Games* are harmful ways we have of making ourselves and others feel bad. We play these games at an ulterior or subconscious level as defenses to protect us from pain which grows from the "not-OK" position.

The "adult" voice or position works best in our family life, our business, our church life, and our social life. The purpose of working through Transactional Analysis or any other method of understanding ourselves is to become more empathetic, to be able to tune in to other persons' feelings. Once we tune into other persons' feelings, we want them to avoid being critical of us and we want to avoid being critical of them. We also want to learn to be adults, so that we can take other persons' comments to us not as criticism, but as helpful suggestions.

How can we use Transactional Analysis in our family and social life? We can begin by avoiding "parent-child" relationships with other adults, and wherever possible, with our children. For example, if you have a child who is late to breakfast, or if your husband is late to supper, rather than raising a great deal of trouble fussing, one could say, "I see you have been late a couple of times. What do you think we should do? Is this going to become a serious problem? Isn't there any way we could work this out so that both of us can be happy with the situation?" You can see that this is a great deal better than fussing and arguing, which will lead nowhere and only let the child in you fight with the child in the other person.

Second, we can give lots of positive "strokes." And above all, avoid stroking a "not-OK" child-like ego-state.

Strokes is another term you need to know in dealing with Transactional Analysis. *Strokes* is taken from the fact that babies are stroked; that is, are given close, warm, repeated bodily contact in order to make them feel affirmed, positive, and secure. As we grow older, recognition by other people and their appreciation of us come to be the psychological version of physical stroking. However, this doesn't mean that many times we do not need physical stroking—a hug or a kiss from our husband or wife, our child, or friend. But normally we receive our strokes psychologically rather than physically as adults.

Positive strokes reinforce OK feelings. That is, positive stroking or appreciation from others makes us feel good about ourselves and allows us to work more efficiently from an OK happy position. Negative strokes reinforce "not-OK" feelings. Someone who is convinced that he is not OK may work for negative strokes to assert himself, that is to assure himself that he is not good—that his opinion that he is bad is a correct one. We can see this working all around us although it may strike us as a bit insane. Many people desire to fail, to be misused, or mishandled. Many people are unhappy with us when we don't abuse them. But it is not very adult or Christian of us to mishandle or abuse them just because it makes them happy. The bad little boy proves to his own satisfaction that he is just as nasty and mean as everyone says he is, by getting negative strokes. But a truly adult controlled personality is not going to continue to feed that kind of sickness.

How do we give strong positive strokes to people around us? Strong positive strokes come from the parent's adult ego-state and they require good eye contact and compliments that are highly specific. Don't say, "Everything about you is great, Jane," but rather say, "I certainly like the color of your dress and the way your hair is fixed, Jane." Be sensitive and be specific. Don't try to be fradulent in your behavior with others, strokes must be sincere.

Third, be aware of the games that children, parents, spouses, and members of organizations often play with each other. It simply wastes time, weakens trust, and destroys all candor and truthfulness.

There are many common games played in our family life

and social situations. One of these games is called "the double bind." The double bind occurs whenever a husband, wife, parent, or child puts another person in a position where whatever they do is wrong. If the person comes early to meals, that person is somehow trying to force the other person to feed him. If the person is late to meals, then he is trying to somehow show that he doesn't like the other person, or the food that is being served. You can see that there is no possible way in which a husband or a wife trapped in a situation like that could satisfy the other. This is a double bind situation. You may smile to yourself and say, this is a very uncommon thing, but you would be wrong, for double binds are the stuff of everyday life and many marriages.

Often-times if a husband works hard and makes a great deal of money, his wife will declare that all he is interested in is money. On the other hand, if the husband doesn't work hard and doesn't make a lot of money, the very same wife might say that he doesn't care about them at all. So whatever the husband does, he has to lose. Of course, husbands do this against wives, too. If a wife takes care of herself and she looks very attractive, a "not-OK" husband may think that she is interested in other men and wants to impress them. But if that wife in order to keep that husband's jealousy in check, lets her appearance go, then the husband might say, "You don't care anything at all about me, you don't take care of yourself, you just slop around the house, and in short, you just make my life miserable." Then it is very clear that fixing herself up won't be an answer for that wife's problem. This is a double bind situation and it is one of the more terrible games that we can play with each other.

One of the other games is "Why don't you—yes, but." This is a game in which one appears to be asking for advice, but has a comeback for every suggestion. Sometimes a neighbor will play this with you. He or she will come over and say, "My son has run away, what do you suggest I do?" You might respond, "Well, let's go check with his friends and see if we can find out where he went?" But the neighbor might come back, "His friends won't talk to me and I don't like them anyhow." Then you'll say, "Let's call the police and see if they can find something out." But the neighbor will respond, "I don't want to bring the police in on this because I don't want to cause my son trouble." And it will go on and on for hours because there is really nothing that is going to be done. All he wants to do is talk about the situation. It is a way in which people feel superior to us because they have an answer to everything we suggest.

There is another common game which is played in the business world. It's also played in the military, at home, and in school many times. We call it "Wooden Leg." In it a person uses a real or an imagined disability as an excuse for not performing an expected duty or obligation. We are all familiar with the story of the wife who tells the husband at bedtime, "I have a headache." There are husbands who have headaches, too. "Wooden legs" crop up again and again. We are familiar with children who can't go to school because their throat is sore, or they feel bad, or they can't sleep. Many times if we check we will see that there is an examination that has been missed, or there is a student there who they are on the outs with, or a teacher who has been giving them a dressing-down, or some other situation that they don't want to face. A person cannot live all his life walking on a wooden leg, when he really doesn't have one. One cannot have a headache every night of the year.

Finally, we can simply say, "Don't play games." The antidote to game playing is to refuse to play the expected game that is offered to you. This means, whenever someone wants you to play "Why don't you—yes, but," you refuse to offer expected advice, or if you are put in a double bind, you simply walk away and refuse either to do good or bad, to turn left or right, for it is clear that if you do anything it will only keep the game going. I think if you do this you will find that your life is happier, and you may help those around you to be happier, too.

Coping with Death

Among the events in life over which we exercise little or no control are the big issues that trouble and convulse society in every generation: economic inflation, business recession, high taxes, unemployment, and the demands of the job as well as the recent social ills of ecological pollution, race problems, and continuing war.

But there are more personal events that are beyond or almost beyond our control: illness, aging, and death.* We can prevent illness, of course, to a certain extent by proper nutrition, exercise, and medical care, but ultimately some sickness or accident comes. And eventually, for all of us, there is death. We need not fear death either as mature persons who know it is a part of life, its last act, or as Christians who know that God is the God of the living and not the dead. We know that in him, there is eternal life. Nevertheless, death does make most of us uneasy. Many of us have not come to the place where we have accepted our death as part of life.

Coming to the Crossroads

Some years ago, while serving as a pastor in Florida, a rough but friendly man entered my church office. He introduced himself as a person who had not been active in the organized church since his youth. Now, in his middle forties, he had undergone radical surgery for stomach cancer. So far, several operations had been unsuccessful in halting the cancer's

---

*A good book to read on aging is Jane Kinderlehrer's *How to Feel Younger Longer* (Rodale Press, Inc., Emmaus, Pa., 1974); see Morton Puner's *To the Good Long Life: What We Know about Growing Old,* (Universe Books, N. Y., 1974); also Reuel Howe's *How to Stay Younger While Growing Older* (Word Books).

On death, read Elisabeth Kubler-Ross *Questions and Answers on Death and Dying* (Collier Books, 1974) and Marjorie C. McCoy, *To Die with Style* (Abingdon Press, 1974).

growth. He frankly feared more surgery and the real possibility of death. Medicine was failing him. This man turned to the church. Let's call my friend Frank. Frank did become my friend. He was not hypocritical nor cowardly, only realistic about his chances. Frank wanted to prepare for death. He knew little of the faith so I gave him adult instruction in the catechism. I loaned him books, visited his home, later received him as a member of the church.

Not long after joining our congregation, Frank died of abdominal bleeding following unsuccessful surgery. I stood by the recovery room bed, in the midst of his ending, handing folded sheets to the doctor who attempted to pack Frank's wounds. Frank looked up at me with startlingly clear eyes and held my hand with more strength than I would have thought possible. We began the Lord's Prayer together. Frank died with its closing words.

I believe this man's faith was genuine. Frank looked for security, for someone to trust, in Christianity. I felt—and still feel—close to this man, who faced eternity with a wistful smile on his face and died without complaining.

In the struggle to survive during the winter of 1950-51 in Korea, I stood by to support a number of men who passed through similar experiences of death. Once I held a young man's hand and tried to calm him through a long night, after he had been struck in the temple by a rifle round. It was very dark and one of his eyes was covered over with a thick emergency dressing. He was afraid that he was blind. We sat in a ditch and waited for morning when a medical jeep would come up to our position. The boy longed for dawn yet feared the coming of the sun, which might well prove that he was blind. Other men, hit in the face and covered with bandages, would deny that they were blind, would not admit that they could not see. The anxiety of being totally helpless in an environment when mortar shells might begin falling at any time was too much for them. But this boy verbalized his fears, calmly yet insistently. He prayed the Lord's Prayer several times. When the light grew strong enough for me to see him clearly, he looked all around with his uncovered eye. He could not see. "I guess that's it," was his only comment.

We need a religious faith that provides us not only with a challenge that shakes us out of our self-centeredness but also with a security and peace that enables us to face illness, disease, blindness, old age, and death. I believe we can find that security in the man God sent, Jesus Christ.

7.

Who Do You Believe?

JOHN C. COOPER

It became evident in chapter six that relationships with others in our families, in our churches, and in our communities formed a most important portion of life. In this chapter we would like to develop the concept that trusting is absolutely vital to the relationships which we have with others and most especially with our God. Christianity is based on faith, after all, sometimes we misunderstand what the nature of that faith is, and in this chapter we would like to make faith a little more clear. Christianity is based on trust, also. If the believer does not trust his Lord, then it is hard to say who, if anyone, the believer trusts. Actually in Christianity, faith equals trust. Trust in God, in that one we call Father, and whom we declare is all-loving, all-caring, all-wise.

Let's talk about love, faith, and trust. Very often faith is understood in American Protestantism and in other forms of Christianity as being somehow a will to believe. It is taken sometimes as a desire to commit ourselves to certain tenets or beliefs. Looking at faith this way equates it to a commitment. Of course, commitment is good. We are not making light of the content of the Christian faith. But what is important to see is that our lives are not based upon a commitment to a set of beliefs or goals, rather our lives are based on trust in God, which means on a relationship of faith with a Living Creator and Savior. Faith in the New Testament is so different from the way we normally use it everyday. We talk about faith, meaning that we believe in baptism, or we believe in sharing, or we believe in forgiving. But when the New Testament talks about faith it uses such expressions as this one from Paul, "Faith is the gift of God." Faith is not something that we make, but that God makes possible in us. Faith is being grasped by the divine Savior. It is being caught up by the Holy Spirit. It is being put in a right relationship with the Triune God. Faith is the basis of Christian faith. And yet so many of us have so little faith in ourselves and in each other, and by extension, perhaps so little faith in God. Perhaps the problems we have in our lives—not just in this middle life—but all through life stem from the weakness of our faith.

Now let's talk a bit about love. Love is something that is widely discussed and we think widely understood. And yet we are always finding disappointments in love. We think of love in the way the Greek philosopher, Plato, thought of *eros*. *Eros* is a form of aspiration, aspiring to reach the heights of ambition. The word *eros* properly falls in the root of the English word "erotic," meaning to be attracted to someone else because of the physical feelings of attractiveness. This is aspiring, perhaps, to become the lover of someone. But it can also be meaning to speak of an erotic or eros-type love, to be attracted to fame, to become well-known. One can also speak of an erotic love of possessions, one loves something—a beautiful home, an expensive car, a place in the country, a trip around the world, or anything, including money. This is the work of *eros* in the world, it is man trying to raise himself up. It is men and women trying to rise to heights whether it be a passion, or fame, or stability and security. *Eros* is something that stems purely from human desires, and is filled with human strength, so it isn't surprising that *eros* often fails.

There is another kind of love that still is not Christian love, but it is a form of love that is noble. This is *philia*. *Philia* is the kind of love talked about by the old Greek philosopher Aristotle, who wrote about friendship. We can see the Greek word *philia* in the root of the English word *philadelphia,* which means brotherly love. *Philos* and *delphos*—love and brother. So that *philia* is brotherly love—it is friendship. It is the kind of love that wishes the best for someone else. A friend is an alter ego. A friend who is another self, so to speak. And yet *philia* also is based upon human love and human strength. It is a strong kind of love because it comes from two parts—friends love for each other—and yet it does not always endure. We know that friends do fall out, and one of the hardest things that we have learned in life, I suppose, is that friends do, sometimes, stop being friends.

The Bible tells us about a different kind of love—stronger than *eros,* which grows out of our ambitions and desires and wants, and stronger even than friendship, which grows out of our more noble sentiments and the interaction between two or more people. It speaks of *agape*. *Agape* is different from the love that starts with humans. It is not a faith, it is not an affection, it is not a noble feeling that we express, rather it is a love that reaches down from above, from God, and embraces us even when we do not deserve it.

The love of God, the word of God, the Christ of God, all of these are *agape*. This is the good news. This is what the word gospel means. To have the good news means that God loves us, and as the Apostle Paul has put it, "At the right time, even when we were still in our sins, the right man dies for us, to atone for us." It is on this love and faith that the Christian is able to have a life of trust.

Now what about trust? Trust means to wholeheartedly give your cares and concerns into the hands of another. Of course, it would be foolish to put your trust in the wrong person. To put your trust in someone who is not finally trustworthy is a terrible thing. We have all lived long enough now to know that these terrible things do happen to us. But we can trust God. This is the message of the New Testament. It's the message that the Hebrew people received in their wanderings and in their trials and sufferings in the Old Testament. God is trustworthy. To know that we can trust the Lord—that is the message of the Scriptures.

But when we turn away from theology and biblical subjects to the every day lives we lead, we find that friendship, love, caring, and intimacy are based on trust, too. Ask yourself, now, silently, honestly: Whom do you really trust? Whose word is a good word in your opinion? Whom do you not doubt at all? Who is it that you know about who you have no doubts? Who has shown you by their faithfulness, by their lovingness, by their trustworthiness, that in them you may place your trust?

Perhaps you would like to take a piece of paper and write down a list. Put a heading by it: "People I Trust." Your list might go something like this: husband or wife; medical doctor; pastor; child or children; the boss; or one of your employees. Your neighbor—or several of your neighbors. Your parents. The man at the gas station where you do your weekly auto servicing—I have had many friends like that that I know I can trust. It could be the postman. Perhaps he is someone who stops and talks with you every day. It could be the policeman who guards your block. It could be almost anyone. But do you trust yourself as well? Think about that. Would you trust someone if they are as trustworthy as you are? Or would you not trust them if they had the same love, faith, trustworthiness, courage, nobility, and selflessness that you have.

After you have written down these people whom you trust —either by title or by their names—describe why you trust them. What are the qualities about them that inspire confidence and trustworthiness in you? You might want to think about this. Perhaps it is the strength of someone. Perhaps it is the calmness of someone. Perhaps it is because you have told them many things quite privately and they have kept your trust. Think about what makes another person trustworthy in your sight, and you may come to some insight as to what you should be like to be trustworthy and trusted by others.

Let's look at the whole angle of faith and trust from this direction now. Write down a list of people whom you believe trust in you. Note that this is a list of people whom you have every reason to believe put their trust in you and have no doubts. Be honest in this evaluation. Who would be on that list? Would your husband or wife? Would your child or children? Would your good friends—perhaps your boy friend—or girl friend? Would your neighbors be on that list? Would your parents? Would your boss—or your employees? Would your doctor be on that list? Would your pastor? Would your Sunday school teacher—or your Sunday school pupils, be on that list? Be honest. How many people do you think really trust you?

Now this isn't meant to be an inquisition. It's an attempt to make you honest with yourself and to look more closely. Think about yourself. Perhaps if you think few people trust you and you trust few people, maybe it's because your life position is wrong. According to the popular psychology known as Transactional Analysis, "life position" means the way we feel about ourselves and others. And it determines to a large extent the kind of transactions or interactions we have with other people. This is the basis by which we either give people positive or negative strokes—we either make their lives pleasant or unpleasant.

Basically there are two ways we can feel about other people and ourselves—OK or Not-OK. A person who feels OK about himself or herself feels that he or she is a worthwhile person. Therefore this person doesn't have to spend a great deal of energy trying to demonstrate to others or to himself that he is, in fact, OK. A person feels OK or not-OK from the child-ego-state. Typically, this very basic feeling is a carry-over from our childhood or formative years. It results from an accumulation of feelings from early contact with our parents which shaped and hardened the way we think and feel about others—a fundamental position that is called "life position." Unfortunately, we make this weighty judgment about ourselves at a time when we are not really up to making it, that is, when we are only children. Unless we later give the matter of how we look at ourselves much thought and make a conscious effort to change this position—in some cases with the help of professional counseling—the position we took when we were children will continue to be part of our lives and will govern our actions ever after.

Ask yourself now, whom did you trust when you were a child? Who did you trust as a teen-ager? Did you have a boy friend or a girl friend? Did you have many boy friends or girl friends? Whom did you trust as a young adult? As a young married person? Whom did you trust on your first job? Or perhaps in the army or other military duty?

We come into this world helpless, unable to feed, clothe, warm, or defend ourselves. We may bawl and cry out, but we are totally dependent upon our parents—and we come to a position of absolute trust in them—if our psycho-history is normal. But perhaps we have been deprived. We know that little children who do not have normal parental affection, even if it is given by nurses or substitutes, often wither and die—if not physically, then something within their spirit dies. Even negative strokes or being fussed at is better than being left completely alone.

We continue to trust our parents through grade school, but in our teens we often come to question them, even to rebel in certain ways. This is not a reason for guilt and shame, in itself, but it is a part of the maturation process. In some the rebellion does go too far for healthy family relations, however.

When did you first question your parents? Do you recall when you first became aware that your mother and father were not infallible or all powerful? How did you feel? Did you think them weak or unintelligent? Did you even begin to despise them? How did you feel about yourself then? Mark Twain remarked that when he was fifteen he knew how dumb his father really was. And at twenty-five he was surprised to learn how much the old man really knew. Perhaps that has been our experience.

When did you leave home? This is a rather important question. Did you leave home early? Or late? Did you leave home to go to college? The armed forces? Or to marry? How did the break away from home make you feel? Did it make you feel adult and important? Or did it make you feel scared, lonely? Did it make you feel proud? Did it make you happy? Or sad? How do you think your parents felt when you left home? What was your relationship to them on the day of your leaving? What was your relationship to your parents after you left home?

How does the memory of your own life history square with your experience with your own children? Or, if you aren't married, with the experiences of your friends and their children? Martin E. Marty has said that we need to search for "a usable future." Perhaps we need to search in time and memory for a "usable past," also. Thinking back upon our childhood, our teen-age, and our young adult years, and of the time when we left home, we can see that there are basically four life positions, any one of which may be ours. It is important to recognize the implication of each of these life positions. They are ways in which we can account for our behavior in our home and at work, and by understanding our behavior we might learn to master our own responses. It should be noted that these life positions operate at a largely subconscious level once we're mature, but they do underlie all our relationships with other people.

The four life positions

1. I'm OK—you're OK
2. I'm not OK—you're OK
3. I'm not OK—you're not OK
4. I'm OK—you're not OK

A person in position #1 (I'm OK—you're OK) is a pleasure to everyone. Unlike the other three positions which were formed in youth, according to the transactional analysts, this one is finally decided upon in maturity. We might say that I'm OK—you're OK is a grown-up way of looking at the world and ourselves. Therein lies the hope for change through conscious efforts by adults who sincerely want to change their lives and to be more trusting of others and more trusting of God, as well as being a more trustworthy person themselves. The I'm OK—you're OK person is free of the basic hang-ups that result from not-OK feelings; he doesn't play psychological games. He is prepared to roll up his sleeves and get on with the work. This winner's position allows him to live up to his capabilities and achieve his objectives. He doesn't have to squander energy on building protective façades and he does not feel compelled to check out the OKness of other people. In short, such an OK person doesn't have to go around telling other people that they are really not OK, and making them feel bad.

What about Your Own Trustworthiness?

Sometimes we may feel that we are caught in an "authority trap" when we reach middle life. What does that mean? It means that we are authorities for our children, for younger people in general, and perhaps for our students or for our employees. But we must also look up to authorities placed over us—our employers, civil officials, the police, the president. Can we fruitfully handle our present situation as the pivot, the hinge or swing point of authority in our society?

Just what is authority? An authority is someone who makes decisions about behavior and future projects and expects us to be obedient to those decisions. An authority may be moral and persuasive, as a parent usually is, and as a pastor or teacher generally is; or he may be (possibly) coercive, that is, he may use his authority backing it up with the force of law—and ultimately with armed force—as in the case of governmental officials or the police. An authority is a "stopping place," a deciding center, one who by knowledge, wisdom, power, or influence is an arbitrator of disputes and a maker of plans for the future. Authority grows out of tradition, on the basis of group decisions, and out of natural power, strength, wisdom, or beauty. Parents inevitably are authorities, as are teachers, pastors, and employers.

Earlier we spoke of the four life positions identified by Transactional Analysis. Now that we are considering our own trustworthiness, let's consider the three life positions that make us less than fully mature, authoritative, and trustworthy people. Notice the lack of self-trust in each one of these "not-OK" positions.

Position #2 (I'm not OK—you're OK) is a kind of servile, self-demeaning stance in relation to others. It is a loser's position. This person feels inferior and is unlikely to attain happiness even if he achieves some success. No matter what happens it is hard for him to feel good about himself. The pleasure of a recent victory quickly gives way to anxiety over the next. He is concerned with the approval of others and may work hard to get it. But even this does not bring lasting satisfaction or relief. Because he does not feel good about himself at heart, he finds it difficult to enjoy compliments about himself or his work. His not-OK "child" fears failure or rejection and throws up its defenses.

Though he may appear at times to be unconcerned about what others think of him or his work, he really cares a great deal. He may have a tendency to withdraw from others. He needs reassurance and recognition, but most of all he needs a friend who demonstrates recognition of his worth as a person apart from his successes or failures. Such a person can progress well under authorities whose predominant style is nurturing "parent" or "adult," but he would be completely stunted under a critical "parent" style. Why? Because he would tend to accept critical "parent" rebukes as a true reflection of his personal worth. The best that he would be capable of producing would probably come from his adapted "child." It would be uninspired, conforming, routine behavior. He would never break out of his shell.

Position #3 (I'm not OK—you're not OK) is extremely difficult to cope with because it is so negative toward self and others. The person who holds it may distrust everyone and see little worth in life and work—certainly a loser's position. It would take someone extraordinarily sensitive, patient, and understanding to get through to such a person. In this as in the other positions there are, of course, degrees of OKness and not-OKness. Extreme, absolute negativity is fortunately the exception and is treated by professional therapists. Where the position is not extreme, a person with understanding and patience can overcome distrust and build confidence. Such an approach is essential in successful supervision of this kind of person. Some so-called hard-core unemployables may be in this category.

Position #4 (I'm OK—you're not OK) is one in which a person feels good about himself but distrusts and may well look down on others. Such a person tends to feel superior to others. Though he is likely to be pushy and offensive towards others, he will react indignantly if efforts are made to correct or change him. Since he finds others not-OK, he tends to drive people away. He also tends to come on in his critical "parent" and to offend the "child" in others. Paradoxically, he plays the persecutor toward others even though he sees himself as a victim of people out to take advantage of him. However, he may come to accept others on a one-to-one basis after a trial period during which he assures himself that they are not out to"get" him. With such a personality, the authority must retain his composure at all times and use his "adult" and "child" appropriately to win the subordinate's respect and allegiance.

It is helpful to engage him in "child–child" transactions of the kind that can release tension and build rapport.

The strength of the life positions probably accounts for a great deal of our difficulty in relating to others. Confronted with extreme not-OKness in a subordinate, we may give up and raise our hands in disgust. The authority who has his own not-OK "child" to contend with is going to find it difficult to bring about change in others in the life positions #3 and #4. He will come up short in dealing with #3, and he will probably be the object of a good deal of persecution and game playing in situation #4.

Fortunately for all of us, these life positions can be reconsidered by the "adult," and with persistence, we can change. We can learn to feel good about ourselves and others and practice new, more appropriate behavior that can make us feel better.

How do you feel about authority? Do you find it easy to accept the authority of others? Hard to accept? Are you uneasy when you are in charge? Or do you handle others (give orders, advice, directions) easily? How do other people respond to your authority? Do you strive to be fair to everyone? Are you democratic or autocratic in your directing the work of others? Do you trust those people to whom you delegate authority?

8.

The One We Can Trust

JOHN C. COOPER

Faith as confidence in God becomes more and more of a necessity for a mentally healthy life as we grow older, but it is a faith in the overriding meaningfulness of the events of the world, not a faith that we will be spared suffering. Thornton Wilder put the real situation of man in history very simply and truthfully in his novel *The Bridge of San Luis Rey*. When the ancient bridge over the chasm fell, it carried the just and the unjust together down to destruction. Those of us who have lived long enough to have witnessed the deaths of many friends and acquaintances, to have suffered auto accidents and fires, to have visited hospitals and asylums know that we all do go down together, moral and immoral. Faith must therefore be a confidence that nothing can shake any longer, like that of Job, who declared: "Though he slay me, yet will I trust in him" (Job 13:15, KJV).

We recognize that it is important to love and trust others, to value love, and to trust ourselves. We do not live alone in the universe, nor would we want to. We are a part of the great human race, cells in a living body in which all are equal in dignity while each has his or her own different contribution to make. If anyone fails in his or her task, the whole of mankind is hurt. If anyone proves untrustworthy, his or her family and friends are damaged. We depend on each other, we need each other, and we are needed.

We know that if we refuse to grow, to change, to assume responsibilities, we cheat many more people than ourselves alone. The parent who deserts the family harms the present and future lives of spouse and children, and hurts the community as well as himself. Other lives depend upon us in the everyday world of home and job, school and play as surely as they do for the soldier in the midst of battle.

No person is an island. Life was not meant to be solitary. We are together in this world and our greatest need is for friendship, caring love, intimacy, trust, belief, faith, and acceptance.

The Christian faith declares that we have this acceptance, this love and care, in One who is worthy of our trust. One we can believe in fully; the Lord of Life, True Man and True God; Jesus Christ. Born of the Virgin Mary, Jesus was crucified under Pontius Pilate. He is a genuinely historical figure. We have only to accept the acceptance we have in Christ.

This book is based upon the insights derived from that faith, the faith of the church in every generation—and still its faith in the changes and challenges of our time.

Why can we trust Jesus Christ? How can we know him and know that we can trust him?

Dr. M. deJonge, professor of New Testament at the University of Leiden, the Netherlands, has written *Jesus: Inspiring and Disturbing Presence* (Abingdon Press, 1974). The answer as to how we can know the Christ is that *we know him in the church.* The Christian church is his Body, he is its Head. his Spirit animates the church—including the group of which you are a part. Whenever you sense your acceptance by other Christians, whenever you feel that someone does care for you, whenever love is shown, intimacy made possible; Christ is there. Wilhelm Herrmann, the German theologian who taught many of the giants of Continental Theology before and after World War I once said:

"I meet Christ at the church door. I see him in the faces of the old people gathered there."

Paul Van Buren, an American theologian, has written that we see Christ in people's faces. It is true. We do. The great reformer Martin Luther also believed this. He wrote that we should all attempt to be "little Christs" to our neighbors. That is how we know Christ, by letting him direct our lives in the way of acceptance, love, concern, helpfulness. The farmer who gives a cup of water to a traveler, the housewife who is kind to a neighbor's child—all are being "little Christs."

Jesus Christ is, then, a positive model for our lives, an example to follow.

Most of us are used to the idea of Jesus' life being a model for our lives. Our ministers and Sunday school teachers have given us Jesus' story from the Gospels as a model and example for our conduct over many years of preaching and teaching. To a degree, this is a truthful presentation. We should wish to be Christlike, yet to some degree it is impossible and even undesirable for us to try to be Christlike in all things. We can be "little Christs" without trying to be Christ himself. Often times we overlook the "I'm OK—You're OK" life position of Jesus and assume a Jeremiah-like, critical and condemning position—a I'm OK—you're not OK or I'm not OK, you're not OK life position towards others and think that is being an example of Christ-likeness. It simply isn't. Jesus condemned sin, evil selfishness, the structures of destruction built into society and religion, but he rarely condemned persons. Jesus did not pretend to be perfect, which is a good guarantee that he was! He ate and drank with sinners, forgave those who were sorry for their sinfulness and comforted those who were hurt by the tragedies of life. Jesus was perfectly human, getting tired, getting angry, weeping, and playing with children—

while others, both rabbis and laymen had no time for such things.

It is amazing what children remember about us as adults. One of my teen-aged daughters, upon seeing a little two-year-old girl, told her mother: "I remember being that age. You taught me to buckle my little shoes by calling the tongue of the buckle a 'lazy stick' and showing me how it fitted into the hole on the strap." One of my students remarked years after he graduated: "I remember thinking how good your classes were because you didn't get upset if I was late sometimes or if people brought coffee to class." Before you can help anyone you must accept them as they are, where they are. You must, in short, love them. That is what Jesus did and does.

But more, Jesus Christ is the Spirit of Power within the church and within us that enables us to become more and more like him. He dwells in our hearts by faith. He makes us to be fashioned more and more in the likeness of himself. Alone and unaided, we cannot imitate Christ; by his Spirit we can increase in faith and love. We will speak more of this later. Being in Christ means much more than affiliating with a church.

Who Jesus Is

The church seems to talk a lot about Jesus Christ. What else would a Christian church talk about? Yet, the question remains, why? Why should we continually recount the life of one who lived two thousand years ago?

You know part of the answer. You have probably read the New Testament with its four-fold story of Jesus. Three of the Gospels present Jesus in much the same way, and are called "synoptics" or Gospels that "see together." The fourth Gospel, John, presents Jesus in a slightly different fashion. Jesus is presented by John as a man under authority in no uncertain terms. John presents Jesus as divine, the Son of God, the Redeemer of the world. In this respect John is the church's Gospel.

But there are real problems in trying to discover who Jesus is. John speaks of a one-year ministry, the synoptics (Matthew, Mark, and Luke) suggest a three-year ministry and give different dates for the Last Supper. We can't be sure if it was a Passover meal or a fellowship meal celebrated before Passover arrived. Mark says little about Jesus' divinity, yet John shows us one who was recognized as divine from the first by John the Baptizer. Yet none of the Gospels are in any doubt about Jesus being the Messiah, the Redeemer, the man sent from God. The general picture of Jesus in the New Testament is that of one sent from God, a man completely persuaded that God was his Father. Jesus felt that his Father had given him a specific purpose to perform: to proclaim the incoming kingdom of God, to win the redemption of men and women from the power of sin.

Jesus was also a man of compassion, one who healed people of spiritual, mental, and physical problems. Above all, he forgave people who felt the agony of their sinfulness. But Jesus never condemned the sinner, he opposed evil itself, showing mercy toward weak people who got mixed up with evil. He shows that mercy toward us today.

Jesus was and is a model of mercy, of true caring. He made friends easily with all kinds of men and women. Jesus saw in everyone the possibility of growth in love, wisdom, and forgiveness. He was a compassionate person. He elevated love to a daily way of life, stressing community. Jesus gathered people together in ever larger groups (four thousand, then five thousand at one sermon), telling them the simple truth that God wanted them to love him and to love one another— instead of keeping a burdensome law and getting wrapped up in too much religious ritual.

But the priests and canon lawyers of the day were frightened by Jesus and rejected him. This saddened him, for it meant persecution and a martyr's death. Jesus was truly human as well as divine. He didn't want to die, but he accepted it because he believed it to be his Father's will. Jesus was an obedient

Son and taught us to be obedient, also. Jesus was neither the younger son who became a prodigal or the older son who became self-righteous. He was obedient.

Most of the Gospel story is devoted to the record of Jesus' last week in Jerusalem. When it was clear that the simple people accepted him (his triumphal entry into Jerusalem), yet the powers of the state and church rejected him, Jesus celebrated the Last Supper with his friends, the disciples. Jesus said that if his friends continued to celebrate this meal among themselves, they could always be certain that he would be personally present with them, communicating to them forgiveness of sins. Today, we still meet together to break the loaf and share the cup, knowing that Jesus Christ is among up, giving us his strength, binding us together in love, washing us clean of our trespasses. Wherever those words of institution are spoken and received in faith, we know Christ's real presence is among us. The Lamb of God that takes away the sins of the world.

After the meal, Jesus was betrayed, arrested, beaten, tried, and condemned. Recently, a French court retried the case of Jesus and decided that it was the Roman government that committed legal murder on Jesus, since they feared any possible leader that arose among a captive people. The Vatican II Council of the Roman Catholic Church also held that the Jewish people as a whole were not responsible for Jesus' death. Christians need to bear this in mind. Jesus was crucified and died. He died forgiving his enemies and remembering his earthly mother, in love.

Think of it! We think so much about ourselves. We worry about our lives. Yet Jesus thought of his enemies, of the thief crucified beside him and of Mary, his mother. In the moment of dying Jesus commended his Spirit to the Father. His love was stronger than death. He overcame even the terrible experience of bearing the sins of the world.

Jesus did not fear death, even though he did not desire it. He accepted it because he trusted that One who is the God of the living, not the dead. Jesus knew that all people live eternally in God's sight. We can close our eyes and give up our Spirit in perfect trust in the God of life.

But the case was not closed. God did not count the story over. Some hours after Jesus' burial several women went to Jesus' tomb and found it empty. These same women, and others of his friends, believed they saw Jesus alive and well—not only on that day but for some forty days thereafter. On the basis of these resurrection experiences, the Christian church was founded. The disheartened disciples found renewed courage and faith. Now the surest thing in the world for these people was the living power of Jesus through whom God had made known his loving will for men. Not just an empty tomb, but lives filled with the living Spirit of Christ made this group the basis of the church.

We are direct inheritors of the disciples' faith, members of the church that grew around the crucified and risen body of Jesus Christ. We are heirs of God, fellow heirs with Christ. Shouldn't we feel OK and loving if we truly have this faith?

Every generation must make a decision about Jesus. We too—you too—must decide who Jesus is going to be for you. Even if you were reared in the church, you must make this decision for yourself. You can't live with a second-hand faith. No one can do your believing or your dying for you. Martin Luther remarked about that 450 years ago. He said we either take Jesus as our Savior, or we leave him alone.

Who Is Jesus? What Can He Be for Us?

Jesus is the living Spirit in the church. He is "God with us," the One who reveals the essence, the heart, of the invisible God. For us, now, Jesus is a way of living in the world, living in love, hope, faithfulness, and kindness. Jesus thus makes it possible for us to achieve our full self-realization. Jesus' living Spirit helps us to realize our own and others' best potential.

Jesus is a way of living and he is also freedom. He sets us

free from bitterness about the past, from crippling self-guilt, from pride and prejudice.

Finally, Jesus is the seal of our forgiveness and of our participation in God's kingdom—eternal life. We know that we shall live because he lives.

Yet, Jesus encourages us to live now, our hope and activity is part of a higher life, an eternal life that begins now, in this world. He challenges us to live now, helping all others, challenging the powers of evil, overcoming depression and lies. Jesus does not call us out of the world but into the midst of its struggle and pain. In this spiritual urgency to live and love now there is the refreshing thought that Jesus accepted everyone without distinction. Thus, Jesus accepts us as we are—clumsy, not brilliant, middle-aged, young, or old. We know that the only thing that counts is what we are like inside, and how willing we are to change and grow with his help.

Being in Christ

Everyone who has read the epistles of Paul is familiar with the phrase, *in Christ*. It is impossible to study that large section of the New Testament, without coming across these two important words again and again. We read of:

> redemption in Christ—Romans 3:24
> baptism in Christ—Romans 6:3
> eternal life in Christ—Romans 6:11
> the love of God in Christ—Romans 6:23
> of being one body in Christ—Romans 12:5
> of being sanctified in Christ—1 Corinthians 1:2
> of being asleep in Christ (in death)—1 Corinthians 15:8
> and that God was in Christ—2 Corinthians 5:19
> as well as of freedom in Christ—Galatians 2:4
> and of Being justified in Christ—Galatians 2:17

Indeed, we read of being in Christ, and of being in the

Lord (a "cognate," or similar term) 164 times in the epistles traditionally ascribed to Paul.

A phrase that is so often used in the New Testament must be an important one—for Paul and for us. And yet, there is no clear idea in the minds of many Christians as to just what Paul meant by our being in Christ. There are several reasons for this, namely, that the outlook of twentieth-century people is quite different from that of Paul's time. Today we have no trouble in conceiving of material things, or of organizations, and so we often consider being in Christ as equal to being in the church. We think, "The church is called the body of Christ by Paul, so when one is in unity with, or 'in,' the church then he is in Christ." This is certainly partially true—indeed being in the body of Christ, the church, is part of what is meant by being in Christ—but it is not all.

The Meaning for Paul

The great Pauline scholar, Adolf Deissmann, has suggested that being in Christ can be interpreted by using the analogy of the way we human beings live in air. Just as all of us live in air and cannot live without it, so the Christian lives in Christ— and cannot live (as a Christian) without him. Also, just as the air is inside all living things, in our lungs and throughout our body, even so, Christ is in the Christian and lives in him. And just as the air refreshes our bodies and gives us newness of physical life, so Christ within us (and we, in Christ) gives us newness of spiritual life. Being in Christ means that we live a life in which Christ surrounds us like the atmosphere which we breathe.

But in what sense are we in Christ and is he in us? Is this simply a metaphor expressing a beautiful thought? Or do we live in Christ only through our knowledge of him gained from our study of the Bible, from sermons, and from worship. Or is he in us only in our memories of Christlike deeds and of spiritual people we have known and loved?

Or could it be that Paul means to say that we are actually in Christ when we are in faith and that his Presence is available to us in our religious experiences of worship, prayer, and meditation? This is the factor in Paul's thought (we may correctly call it the mystical or spiritual factor) which is difficult for us, with our modern outlook on the world to understand. But it is exactly what St. Paul means by using the phrase, "in Christ."

Paul is using the phrase "in Christ" to refer to an experience which he and all other Christians have had, and continue to have—the experience of a spiritual Presence. Paul speaks of Christ as present with him now, not just as a memory (in our modern sense) from the past, but as a participation, a fellowship, now. It is not a physical presence, but a spiritual one—although Paul speaks of the presence of his Lord in a quasi (half) physical way, as was the custom of the time. Paul was so convinced that Christ stood next to him and lived in him, guiding his life, that he felt forced to speak of the Lord's spiritual presence in almost physical terms. For example: "I know a man in Christ . . . " (2 Corinthians 12:2).

And the crowning passage: "I have been crucified with Christ; it is no longer I who live, but Christ who lives in me; and the life I now live in the flesh I live by faith in the Son of God, who loved me and gave himself for me" (Gal. 2:20).

For Paul, if a man is a Christian, accepts Christ as his Savior, and trusts in him alone, then that man will lead a life that will grow into a deeper and deeper "mystic union" or inner communion with his Lord. This inner communion with God through faith in Christ is the internal side of the Christian's life, and it goes hand in hand with the believer's external communion with the body of Christ, the church, and with its individual members. This union, both with the Lord in one's innermost self, and with the church, as the expression of Christ's love and service on earth, is present from the very beginning of the Christian life—in baptism. As one grows older this communion with the Lord (being in Christ) becomes clearer as one becomes more aware of it—through the example of Christlike people, through Scripture study, and through one's own experiences in time of trouble and time of prosperity, which issue in a reliance upon prayer.

For Paul, and for us, there is a spirit let loose in the world—a spirit of healing, of power, of goodness, of justice, and of love. Paul thought of that spirit as filling the world and of filling us. Christ is always there, Paul seems to say. Only we, in our crass materialism and spiritual blindness may not be aware of him. Paul tells us clearly, God loves and forgives us—accept his love and acceptance of you.

Why Speak of Being in Christ?

For Paul, being in Christ is simply the outgrowth of what Jesus Christ has done. Paul saw the decisive element in the Christian faith to be the manifestation of the Divine in the world, the Incarnation of the Christ, Jesus of Nazareth. And not only did God reveal his love and power in Jesus' life, but he also carried through a series of divine actions that changed the course of history. Christ had died on the cross and risen from the dead, and in so doing had broken down the barriers of estrangement that separated sinful men from God, and this forgiveness was available to all who believed in Christ's atoning death. Thus Jesus Christ had shown that God was a gracious and loving Father who freely gave us all that righteousness the Law demanded but could not give. That was the objective, once for all, work of Christ. And here, the missionary preacher, Paul, in 55 A.D. faced the same problem of understanding and communication that we face in trying to witness to our faith in 1976 A.D.

The Meaning for Us

How is this justification or reconciliation to be made operative and applied to human lives in generations after the life and work of Christ? Paul worked several decades after the life of Christ, and thus faced the same problem we face, trying to make the external fact of redemption internal in the life of the believer. He had to see how the objective fact of Christ's atonement is made subjective—received for and by us. To make this connection, Paul had recourse to the traditional Jewish theological language about the Holy Spirit or the spirit of the Lord. Here he saw the living connection between the act of Christ on the cross and the act of God in the resurrection event, and the act of faith at the Christian-removed-from those decisive acts in time and space. Thus Paul speaks of the risen, living Christ as "the Spirit" (2 Cor. 3:4 f; 3:17–18). This does not mean that Paul had no doctrine of the Holy Spirit (as distinct from the spirit of Christ), but it does mean that Paul had no fully developed trinitarian doctrine, and that he seems to be unclear in his own mind as to the precise identity of the Spirit and of his place in the Godhead. This is only to be expected, as Paul was the first theologian, and the doctrine of the Holy Spirit was not fully settled until late in the fourth century A.D.

Paul gives us evidence that he at times thought of the Spirit as the extension of the personality of God the Creator (Father) into the world; and at other times, he speaks of the Spirit as a more or less distinct divine Presence. But in the majority of times, Paul speaks of the Spirit as the way in which the Presence of the Risen Christ is mediated to the believer.

Thus, it is Paul's belief in the real presence of the spiritual Christ that lies beneath the phrase "in Christ." We are in Christ because Christ truly is here in the midst of life with us, and we are in him, in a deeper more genuine sense than that of simply belonging to the church. We are in Christ because the Christ-Spirit is in the world, manifesting divine power, healing and helping us even now. For he who died for the sins of the world and rose again is alive now, reigning, unacknowledged by sinners, in the world-at-large, and reigning, acknowledged and adored, in the believer's heart, by the power of Almighty God.

I began this book by suggesting that we people in the

middle have more and more of the need for a confidence in
God as our responsibilities grow. As we grow older, we certainly grow more humble. We become aware that we cannot
do everything, we become aware that we will not last forever.
We become more aware of our need for that One whose
strength is sufficient for us and whose faithfulness is unchang-
ing. Therefore, it is not sentimentality but the very logic of
maturity that makes us say, "We, too, believe in Christ . . .
we, too, wish to live in his spirit."

JOHN C. COOPER is dean of academic affairs and professor of systematic theology at Winebrenner Theological Seminary. Prior to assuming this position, he was chairman and professor of philosophy at Eastern Kentucky University. Dr. Cooper received the B.A. degree from the University of South Carolina, the M.Div. from Lutheran Theological Seminary, the S.T.M. from the Lutheran School of Theology, and the M.A. and Ph.D. from the University of Chicago. John Cooper is the author of sixteen previous books, including **Religion After Forty, Finding a Simpler Life,** and **Fantasy and the Human Spirit.** He and his wife, Ann, have four children: Chris, Cathy, Cindy, and Paul.

RACHEL CONRAD WAHLBERG is currently a freelance writer. She has taught English at Armstrong Junior College in Savannah, Georgia, and at Salem Academy in Winston Salem, North Carolina. She has traveled extensively throughout the United States and abroad speaking and writing on the subject: "The Changing Image of Women in the Church and Society." Rachel received the A.B. degree from Lenoir Rhyne College and the M.A. in English Literature from the University of Virginia. Rachel and her husband, Phil, have four children: David, Aumla, Pauli, and Sharon. She is the author of **Leave a Little Dust** and **Jesus According to a Woman.**